The Toff
and the
Great Illusion

John Creasey

PRESTIGE BOOKS • NEW YORK

THE TOFF AND THE GREAT ILLUSION

First published in the United States of America in 1967 by Walker &
Company, a division of Publications Development Corporation.
All rights reserved. No part of this book may be reproduced or trans-
mitted in any form or by any means, electronic or mechanical, including photocopying, recording or by any information storage and
retrieval system, without permission in writing from the Publisher.
Printed in the U.S.A.

PRESTIGE BOOKS INC. • 18 EAST 41ST STREET
NEW YORK, N.Y. 10017

NOT LETHAL?

Rollison began to gulp; there was too much dust and he didn't have time to breathe. He had to have air, or collapse. He tried to get to his feet, but someone's knee pushed him in the back, and he fell forward again. He knew that he was suffocating . . .

. . . and then he regained consciousness, not knowing where he was. He was aware only of a great thirst.

He was on the floor of a small bedroom. There was barely room for him between the bed and the fireplace. The room smelled frowsy.

He realized that he was wearing just his underwear, and struggled erect, looking about for his clothes. Then he saw the woman on the bed.

She was very dead.

And the door was locked from this side!

The Toff
and the
Great Illusion

CHAPTER I

THE TALKATIVE
YOUNG LADY

"Yes, of course," said the Hon. Richard Rollison, "yes
. . . really? . . . Oh, I see . . . no, I hadn't . . . yes . . .
yes . . ."

Near the sideboard in the small dining-alcove of his
Gresham Terrace flat, Jolly, his manservant, was pol-
ishing silver and looking towards him in commiseration.
The telephone had rung twenty minutes before, and at
first Rollison had been loquacious; obviously the charming young lady at the other end of the wire had taken
that as a sign that she could gossip indefinitely. Rollison's
responses had become increasingly monosyllabic, and
from time to time he glanced desperately about him, for
he was interested in nothing that Georgina Scott had to
say. He wondered why he had even agreed to speak to
her, and considered the possibility of ringing off. If he
did that, however, she would doubtless ring through
again and give him her opinion of telephones.

"Really!" he exclaimed. "I think . . ."

But she interrupted, and it was long past the time
when he could remind himself that she was a person of
considerable charm.

After another five minutes she said:

"Oh, and Rolly, I simply must tell you about . . ."

" 'Gina, it's getting on for six, and I—" began Rollison, only to hear her exclaim as if in horror:

"Six! Rolly, you shouldn't have kept me talking like
this; I must be out by half-past. I—"

"Then we'd better say good-bye," said Rollison,
straightening up.

"Rolly, don't go! I knew there was something I
wanted to tell you about. I've just remembered it. It's ab-

solutely absurd, of course. I know you won't believe a word of it; but I thought you ought to *know*. It was yesterday—no, the day before. At the Carlton—wait a minute, it might have been at the Savoy, *where* did I lunch? —oh, I remember. I was with Teddy; we went to the Savoy and he had forgotten to book a table—the ape—so we had to wait for nearly half-an-hour, even the Grill was crowded, and we were having an aperitif. It—"

"If you have to be out by half-past six," said Rollison, "you'll have to tell me about this another time."

"No, Rolly. Rolly! You haven't gone? . . . oh, I thought they'd cut you off. It's about you, you see. He didn't look at all the type, either. Teddy pointed him out to me, because of the funny way he talked—out of one side of his mouth, it made him look positively *sinister*."

Rollison felt a kindling of interest.

"Teddy said it's the prison lisp, or something, and that the man must have been in prison for a long time to talk like that," rattled Georgina. "He didn't speak very loudly, but just as we were passing him—there was a free table at last—I heard him mention your name. Wasn't that remarkable?"

"Yes," conceded Rollison, cautiously. "What did—?"

"I just can't remember what he said," confessed Georgina, "but I know he'd been talking about someone he said he'd like to murder—he wasn't laughing, either; he looked really *evil*. Oh, I remember! 'Another of them is Rollison.' Those are his actual words. We were both *starved*, or we would have come to see you or telephoned you at once. Teddy had to catch the 2.15, poor dear, and he made me promise not to forget to tell you, but I've been so busy—Rolly! It's nearly ten past, I must fly!"

"But what did he look—" began Rollison urgently.

"Rolly, I *can't* tell you now! I'll see you some time; of course, there isn't anything in it, really, but you'll admit that it *was* queer. Good-bye!"

" '*Gina!*'" cried Rollison.

He heard the receiver replaced and pictured Georgina, slight and shapely, and given to wearing flimsy dresses which flared about nice legs, rushing away from the telephone. She was always late, and always forgiven because of her looks.

Rollison replaced his receiver and lit a cigarette, eyeing Jolly absently.

"How long was I talking?"

"Over twenty-five minutes, sir," said Jolly, a doleful man to look at, with a deeply lined face and sad, brown eyes. His thinness made him look taller than his five feet eight. "At least, the call lasted for that time. It was Miss Scott, sir, wasn't it?"

"Yes," said Rollison. "She talked all that time about nothing, and then couldn't wait to tell me what she really rang up to say."

"It is quite infuriating, sir."

"It's more," said Rollison. "A man with a prison lisp waiting to lunch at the Savoy and naming me amongst others whom he would like to murder. Miss Scott didn't tell me what he looked like, and even had she tried she would probably have described a man she was sitting next to in the train three weeks ago." He paused.

"It's just possible that the man Miss Scott overheard was talking about someone else of the same name," reflected Jolly, comfortingly.

"It's even probable," admitted Rollison. "If it weren't for the fact that Charmion was released from Dartmoor a fortnight ago, I'd think nothing of it."

Jolly's face dropped.

"Charmion!" he exclaimed, and, by losing his composure even so slightly, robbed the name of all its attractiveness. "I had no idea, sir, I thought—"

"You thought that he would be away for another year," interrupted Rollison. "So did I. Apparently he was quite a hero during an outbreak of fire at Dartmoor, and had an extra year of his sentence remitted. Grice told me last week."

"It *is* disturbing, sir," said Jolly. "I think I would rather it were any man but Charmion. I suppose it is possible that Miss Scott saw someone else?"

"The only hint she gave me about his appearance was that he 'didn't look the type'," said Rollison, "and presumably she meant the type who would talk murder. It fits Charmion."

He stubbed out his cigarette, stepped to the sideboard, and poured himself a whisky and soda.

He was tall, dark and a handsome man. His face was tanned from much tennis and cricket, but the only thought in his mind as he sipped his drink and contemplated Jolly was of Charmion.

He had fought and defeated Charmion more than seven years ago, but the reprieve was not long enough. He had searched the papers for three days after Charmion's release to see whether there were any mention of it; there had been none. A man whose trial had lasted for fifteen days, and who, until the last moment, had appeared likely to get off scot-free after a series of the most beastly, barefaced, but brilliantly conceived crimes, was no longer worthy of mention.

"How old would he be now, sir?" asked Jolly.

"He was thirty-five then," said Rollison. "Oh, he's in his prime."

A picture of Charmion was in his mind's eye.

Charmion was not easy to describe, although his face remained clear in Rollison's memory—a lean, olive-complexioned face with languorous brown eyes, dark hair which fell in waves across his forehead, sensuous lips which curved in a smile so attractive that many of the women had been eager accomplices rather than victims. Charmion had based his defence upon the fact that he had never found it necessary to persuade a single 'partner' to subscribe a penny to his fantastic fund; the money had been subscribed willingly—there had even been competition to get on the list.

That had been true enough; only the fact that he had amassed a fortune of a quarter of a million pounds from the foibles of wealthy women and foolish men had made his success noteworthy.

He had declared that he had promised them nothing

10

for their money; and that, also, had been true. He had instituted a cult called the League of Physical Beauty, and it had become a religion to a minority of people whose names had been household words. In efforts to evade all unpleasant publicity some had made it difficult to get the evidence needed to condemn Charmion. He had dabbled in the occult, but not deeply enough to make it a police matter—only just enough to attract and then to fascinate the women who joined him in his 'crusade.'

One girl, whom Rollison had known well, had joined the League and soon afterwards killed herself. All that was known was that she had become a hopeless drug addict. So Rollison had set himself to prove Charmion's responsibility, while the police had set themselves to prove that the League was nothing but a money-making swindle. They had succeeded without proving that it was illegal; Rollison had traced the drugs to Charmion and thus brought about his final undoing.

There was, however, much more than that.

There was the indefinable atmosphere in which not only Charmion himself was absorbed but into which he had snared many others; he had that quality which was almost hypnotic, and which had made fifty women whose reputations had been at stake step into the box to defend him. In the dock, Charmion had stood without moving, a faint smile on his lips, the lock of wavy hair over his forehead and just touching his right eye. He had believed that he would triumph. Only towards the end, while the Toff had been working in desperation and when the police were pesuaded to use the evidence which he had found, had Charmion faltered.

Rollison remembered how, when he had been in the witness-box, giving evidence which had sent this man to Dartmoor Charmion had stared at him, tight-lipped, his eyes smouldering with a deathless hatred. Rollison had been conscious of it at the time; and the memory of the old tension was very vivid as he finished his drink and lit another cigarette.

"What will you do, sir?" asked Jolly.

11

"I don't quite know," said Rollison. "I'd better see Miss Scott and get her to describe the man. If it were Charmion . . ." he shrugged. "Oh, I don't think there's much doubt, he would have nerve enough to go to the Savoy. He'd be prison-cropped, and wouldn't be easily recognized." Rollison narrowed his eyes and looked towards the ceiling. "The most significant thing is that he had a confidant at the Savoy. What else has he got, Jolly! Money—that's reasonably certain, not a tenth of his profits were found. Friends—?" he paused.

"It's hard to believe, sir," said Jolly.

"Is it?" asked Rollison. He shrugged his shoulders. "Oh well, it will work itself out. I think I'll dine at the Club, but I'll be back before midnight."

"Very good, sir," said Jolly.

He was impassive, but Rollison knew that he was deeply concerned.

Rollison felt irritated, almost exasperated, with the half-formed fears in his own mind. Of all the criminals he had met, Charmion had caused him the most anxiety. It was no novelty for Rollison to be threatened with vengeance; he was the butt of such threats at least as frequently as the higher officers of Scotland Yard, and he was no more perturbed than they. There was no real reason why he should regard this threat differently; perhaps he did so because it had been so vague. Knowing Charmion, he could not believe that the man had allowed a careless sentence to be overheard; he did not make mistakes of that nature. It was far more likely he had known that Georgina Scott and her Teddy—it would be Teddy Marchant, well known to be a friend of the Toff's—would probably pass on the tit-bit of gossip.

That would be typical of Charmion.

The man would do nothing direct; he would simply allow a rumour to leak out here, a hint to pass there, making sure that they would reach Rollison. He would remain in the background, with that obscure smile on his red lips, that strange immobility of feature, mocking, disparaging, disdainful—and dangerous.

"This is ridiculous!" said Rollison to himself as he left Gresham Terrace and walked towards Piccadilly. "I'm not—"

He did not use the word 'frightened'; for he was not frightened, but he was keyed up, and disturbed because so slight an incident had been enough to make him apprehensive and watchful. Had it not been for Georgina Scott, he would not have looked about him to see whether he were being followed, and would not have been suspicious of a middle-aged man who walked behind him the whole way and reached the Circus a few seconds after him.

Almost against his will he crossed the road to the gates of the Green Park. It was dusk; the evening of a perfect day in early spring shed a subdued light about the traffic and the great gates with their statues reaching towards the darkening sky. The noise of the cars and buses was dulled; the park, stretching out in front of him, had the loveliness of the earth awakened from its winter sleep and preparing to greet the first caressing overtures of spring.

Three times he looked over his shoulder; on the last occasion, he did not see the man. He was surprised at the way his heart leapt and his stride lengthened; it was as if major fears had been dissipated. When he reached his Club, in Carlton House Terrace, he was prepared to laugh at himself until, glancing into the park again as an attendant greeted him, he saw the middle-aged man stroll past, bowler-hatted, and with a furled umbrella swinging gently from his arm. The man did not look into the entrance-hall, but walked straight past.

"What did you say, sir?" asked the attendant.

"I've changed my mind," said Rollison, with a fleeting smile. "I'm getting forgetful?" He turned and swung out of the Club in the wake of the bowler-hatted man.

CHAPTER II

THE TRIALS
OF A WITNESS

The man who had caused Rollison so much concern vanished in the evening air. As Rollison did not see him again after leaving the Club, he was more than ever convinced that the trailing had been deliberate.

There was nothing surprising in his decision to dine, not at the Carillon Club, but at Joe's, in the Mile End Road.

To the casual observer, the contrast between the almost sacrosanct Club and the dilapidated, bomb-blasted East End restaurant was as great as that between Buckingham Palace and the Whitechapel Gallery. Very few people know that there was just one thing in common: the Club and the restaurant each had a French cook. True, the Club's chef wore a white smock and a tall white hat and had innumerable assistants, while the fat, shiny-faced Frenchwoman who had married Joe Link during the Great War was lucky if she were able to keep a girl to help her with the washing-up. Yet Rollison, no mean judge, considered that Fifi Link was at least as good a cook as the Carillon Club's chef. Even if she and Joe had to work until midnight, the restaurant, especially the little private room at the back, would be scrupulously clean.

Perhaps because of the black-out, Joe's was practically empty when Rollison reached it. By then, it was quite dark outside; there were few people about, and little traffic, although buses rumbled along the main road and shook the weather-boarding which took the place of windows at the restaurant. A warm, appetizing smell greeted Rollison. No one seated on the high-backed benches of the eating-house looked up, although a man standing at the far end, near the serving-hatch, straightened up and stared through the murky yellow light coming from low-wattage, unshaded bulbs.

The man by the hatch, who was large and unwieldy, wearing a green baize apron and smoking a charred pipe, sprang forward. As he did so, he shouted:

"*Fi!*" making it sound like '*Fee*,' and waddled with unexpected speed towards Rollison, who smiled widely and gripped the moist hand smacked against his own. "*Fi!*" cried Joe Link again, his beam splitting his fat face in two and revealing perfect dentures.

"I am busee," called a woman from beyond the hatch. "Why do you call me, Shoe?" She pronounced it 'Show'.

"Mr. Ar, Mr. Ar, Mr. Ar!" cried Joe, "bless me black 'eart, ain't it good ter see yer! Fi! It's Mr. Ar!" He gripped the Toff's elbow and led him towards the hatch; the door opened quickly, and Fi appeared, short and fat, with magnificent dark hair sternly confined in a net, full lips muttering a French imprecation under her breath. Then she saw Rollison; the frown faded, her eyes gleamed and she held her arms wide.

"Shoe, imbecile, why did you not tell me! M'sieu Roll-'son, this ees a delight, a delight! Well! 'Ow long ees eet? Two years, yes, all of two years. You are not dead, no? *Bien!* M'sieu, you 'ave chose the night of nights. Fish! Such a piece of 'alibut you 'ave not tasted since you last come here, no? Shoe! Take M'sieu Roll'son into the othair room, 'urry 'urry. Soon we close, m'sieu, then you tell us everything *hein?*"

"Fifi, you're prettier than ever," said Rollison, and was rewarded by a delighted clucking as Fifi hurried to finish serving the last of the meals in the restaurant, and Joe took Rollison into the small private room. There he bent down, grunting as he unlocked a small cupboard and brought out a bottle of pernod.

They sipped and talked for twenty minutes, while Fifi's voice could be heard in the outer room—apparently she was sending a girl to collect the plates and start the washing-up. There was a smell of grilling fish, an insidious, gratifying odour.

After pouring Rollison another drink, Joe began to set the table; silver glistened and damask shone, for he had spent a long time as a waiter in the West End. The little room, its walls covered with photographs and cheap prints, ornaments in every available space, a small harmonium against one wall, a sofa and six upholstered chairs, seemed to grow more spacious. Joe hovered about as if he were waiting upon royalty, chattering freely.

Fifi entered, bearing a tureen; she sat with them while they had soup, then hurried to finish serving the fish. Her face grew redder and her voice more shrill, but there was triumph in her eyes when she presented the *pièce de résistance*. It was a triumph.

The conversation might have surprised Rollison's friends at the Carillon and elsewhere, but it did not flag. Rollison learned what had happened to a hundred acquaintances in the East End, heard of the death of a man here, a woman there, of numerous younger men in one or other of the theatres of revolt and revolution; he felt warmed and contented, almost forgetful of the purpose of his call.

Fifi and Joe whipped the dirty dishes from the table, and Fifi returned with coffee and brandy. She switched on an electric fire and set the bowl-shaped glasses before it to warm, then sat down, put her elbows on the table, and beamed.

"Eet ees a delight," she repeated, "but, m'sieu, you are a busee man, you come for some reason, *hein?*"

"See 'ere, Fi," protested Joe, "Mr. Ar don't want—"

"Imbecile!" Fifi exclaimed. " 'Ave you not the eyes? I 'ave seen M'sieu Roll'son thinking, but not about Fifi and Shoe *all* the time. Is that not so, m'sieu?"

Rollison tapped the ash from a Sobranie cigarette, and said easily:

"Yes, Fifi, there's something on my mind."

"You see?" Fifi waved her hands expressively. "M'sieu Roll'son, 'e does not come to waste ze time of 'ard-working folk or 'is own time. For some reason 'e come. M'sieu, speak, please!"

Joe was making frantic efforts to catch Rollison's eye, making it clear that he knew Rollison wanted to talk to him in confidence and that he understood Fifi might be *de trop*.

"Stop it, Shoe!" snapped Fifi, with some annoyance. "I am a grown woman, I do not need to go in the corner. Eh, m'sieu?"

"Now listen—" began Joe.

"I don't know that there's anything very much," said Rollison, leaning back in his chair and raising one eyebrow slightly. "Do you remember, Joe, seven or eight years ago, when you had a waitress named—"

" 'Ilda!" exclaimed Fifi.

"Yes, that's right." Rollison was genuinely surprised. "I'd forgotten her name, but—"

He did not want to frighten them, and knew that they might be alarmed by mention of Charmion. He had come because the waitress, Hilda—at the time of the trial a girl of seventeen of a startling beauty—had been one of his chief witnesses against Charmion. Had he been asked why he was anxious now to find out what he could of Hilda, he would have found it difficult to answer; but he did not find it hard to read the expressions on the faces of Fifi and Joe.

Their smiles had gone.

Fifi's face grew hard, her expression baleful. Joe rubbed his clean-shaven upper-lip slowly, and stared at Rollison from narrowed eyes. The warmth of the party had faded, memory of the meal vanished, the waiting brandy glasses were forgotten. A cold wind seemed to creep into the room, affecting them all.

"So," said Fifi, shrugging. "Eet ees not my image, Shoe."

"O' course it is," declared Joe, sending another appealing glance towards Rollison, "You've got an imagination something chronic. Mr. Ar, don't you take no notice of—"

17

"Are we all fools?" cried Fifi. "'Ere, we are worried for 'ow long? Three, four weeks, about poor 'Ilda. Then M'sieu Roll'son come and inquire of 'er. That is two and two, ees it not? Do not try to 'oodblind me, Shoe. M'sieu, what ees eet you know of 'Ilda?"

"Nothing," said Rollison. "I came to find out what you know about her."

"*There!*" exclaimed Joe, his eyes brightening. "It's just becorse Mr. Ar knew—"

"Silence!" snapped Fifi. "M'sieu, forgeeve Shoe, 'e ees not always the fool like this. 'Ilda, yes, you would like to know of 'er. M'sieu, eet ees not good. She ees married, 'Ilda, weeth three children, such good children, the last one only a year old. Already 'e ees walking, just beginning, you should see 'im. And laugh! 'Ow 'e laugh! That ees Jean." It was her best effort at pronouncing 'John,' but succeeded no better than with 'Joe.' "There ees Dorees, 'oo is four, an' Charl-ee, 'oo is—'ow much, Shoe?"

"Six," said Joe, "but—"

"'Er man, 'e fights," said Fifi. "'E was in Cyprus, *le* pauvre, and then 'e go to Aden, an' later to Borneo. Until then, 'ow long, Shoe?"

"It'd be about six months," said Joe, glumly.

"So, siss months. Until then, 'Ilda, she ees very happy, m'sieu. 'Er man goes, she ees sad. But she puts her children into a nairsery, and goes to work. That ees like 'Ilda, she never was a lazy one, eh, Shoe?"

"No," admitted Joe.

Fifi drew a deep breath, then pouted and exhaled; her eyes were clouded and her hands were heavy upon the table.

"From then, m'sieu, she 'as trouble. An accident, when she ees coming 'ome in the black-out, just a little accident but she says to Shoe an' me, 'I was pushed'. That is so, m'sieu, an' 'Ilda, she would not image that. Then, she ees robbed. Et was not a lot of monnee, but eet was a big loss to 'Ilda. Little theengs, you say? But wait, m'sieu! 'Er Charl-ee, 'e plays in the street, an' 'e ees run over. The man who ees in the car does not stop. Only the good God saved Charl-ee from worse than 'e suffered, *le pauvre*, but now—m'sieu, the doctairs, they say 'e weel not walk proper again."

Rollison felt a constriction at his breast, a sense of horror which the story alone could not have created, but only the background of Charmion; for such horrors as these the mind of Charmion might conceive in his quest for vengeance.

"Is there anything else?" Rollison asked.

Fifi's face was twisted and there was hatred in her eyes.

"M'sieu, eet ees a wicked thing. Only three days ago, now, 'Ilda was returning from her work. She ees at overtime, you understand, and she gets 'ome so late. Eet ees dark, and the streets are mysterious by night, m'sieu, you will know 'ow. Two men, they attack her. 'Ilda, she fights and struggles and screams, she knows that they would seduce her, she ees a good girl. They take the clothes from 'er, and they tie up her mouth, yes, but— m'sieu, there is a good God!—someone had heard her cries, and the police, they come. She was saved from much, m'sieu, but—now she ees in bed. The doctair, 'e says that eet ees shock. The beasts, they kicked and beat 'er when they 'ear the police." There was a moment of silence, broken only by Joe's heavy breathing, and then Fifi jumped up from the table and clapped her hands together. "So, m'sieu. Ees that by accident? Or ees *Charmion* free?"

Into the name she put such depth of feeling that it seemed to hover about them. All the charm it possessed was gone; she made it seem an ugly, horrible thing.

"Or ees *Charmion* free?" she demanded again. "Answer, please!"

"He is," said Rollison, gravely.

"So! Shoe, I was sure; you call it imagine, but I, Fifi, 'ere in my 'eart I felt it." She placed a beringed hand upon her breast. "*Charmion*. Why does not God lay hand upon the man an' strike 'im dead?"

"He's only been out for a few days," Rollison said. He was deliberately flat-voiced.

Fifi looked at him wide-eyed, Joe fingered his upper-lip and did nothing to ease the tension. He expected Fifi to burst out with some excited comment, but it was Jóe who pushed his chair back and spoke.

" 'E ain't alone, is 'e? 'E's got friends, powerful friends, if you arst me. I been trying to tell Fi that there's nothing in it, but it ain't no good, Mr. Ar. I *knows* it's Charmion. I've 'ad a feeling ever since things started ter go wrong with 'Ilda. There ain't a nicer kid in London but —what can anyone do against Charmion, Mr. Ar? Why, if I was ter go to the dicks, they'd larf at me. That's wot they'd do—just sit back an' larf at me!"

"Perhaps that ees so," said Fifi, her voice surprisingly mild. "But there ees M'sieu Roll'son, who does not laugh. M'seiu, you can do something, yes? You are already working, perhaps, against Charmion? That ees why you 'ave come, of course. M'sieu, you will need to be careful."

There was something touching about a faith which he could not betray, even if it were in his mind to try. Fifi's eyes, brown and wide and intense, were turned towards him, Joe's eyes were narrowed; he looked a great hulk of a man, she a fat slattern. He knew them for what they were, knew the depth of their feelings.

Could they all be wrong?

The great fear at the back of Rollison's mind was that these things had happened to Hilda so that he should get to hear of them. Charmion would not waste time and effort, nor take risks for himself, and his accomplices, for so insignificant a person as Hilda. He would aim high; he would probably consider the Toff big game.

What Rollison liked least about it was that the initiative was with Charmion; he had to wrest it from him.

His first problem was to find the man.

CHAPTER III

THE NERVE WAR
GROWS APACE

Rollison did not go to see Hilda, but returned to Gresham Terrace, where he told Jolly what he had heard. One of the things which Joe had said lingered in his mind—the probability that the police would laugh at the story. It was true that they might laugh at Joe, but not at him.

Jolly said, with an almost uncanny insight:

"When will you see Superintendent Grice, sir?"

"Get him on the 'phone, will you?" He went to his bedroom and, while Jolly was dialling a number, took a suitcase from a drawer at the foot of his wardrobe, and carried it into the large room which surprised many people who entered it. One long wall was covered with souvenirs. His friends declared that it showed a morbid, even macabre tendency to display the weapons which had featured in many criminal *causes célèbres*; Jolly certainly disapproved. It was not that Rollison had any affection for the things; they merely fascinated him.

He put the suit-case on the desk, then looked at a small glass case on a shelf plugged into the wall. Inside were the phials containing cocaine—phials which had helped to prove the charge of trafficking in drugs against Charmion. There were others in the Black Museum at Scotland Yard.

Hilda Brent (at the time her surname had been Morgan) had handled those phials, but had been warned in time not to touch the contents.

Jolly was a long time getting Superintendent Grice.

Rollison opened the case; it contained manila folders in which were press-cuttings and other documents relating

21

to various cases; he found the one referring to Charmion's and a large photograph of the man.

All that he remembered about Charmion was there, and more besides; on the right cheek, beneath the eye, there was a small mole. He checked the official police description, and found the mole noted there, set the photograph aside and read through the newspaper reports of the trial. The sober *Gazette*, never a paper to pander to the desires of a sensation-loving public, reported it almost verbatim. Rollison looked for the report of the last day's hearing, and towards the end of it, he read:

"Counsel for the defence, cross-examining Chief Inspector McNab, repeatedly asked whether the police had obtained the information about cocaine themselves, or whether they were relying on the evidence of a private individual, and whether that private individual might not, because of his personal animosity towards the defendant, be likely to produce evidence not wholly reliable?

"Chief Inspector McNab reiterated that the evidence had been obtained by the police with the assistance of the Hon. Richard Rollison, and that evidence had been thoroughly sifted before it had been presented.

"And later, throughout the last stages of the trial, it was noticeable that the accused paid no heed to what was being said, but looked towards Mr. Rollison, who was in court only for a short time."

Rollison remembered the hushed silence when the jury had returned after considering its verdict, and that three women had fainted when the foreman had said: "Guilty, my lord."

Charmion had not fainted; he had looked at Rollison, his expression quite implacable.

"Oh, confound it!" exclaimed Rollison. "Seven years ago! What the devil's got into me?" He looked up as Jolly entered. "Have you got him?"

"No, sir. He's not at his home, nor at the Yard. No one appears to know where to find him."

"I'll try myself later," said Rollison.

He did not succeed in getting in touch with Grice, however, and went to bed, his mind confused. One part of it argued, unconvincingly, that there was really no evidence that Charmion was responsible for what had happened to Hilda, and that the remarks Georgina had overheard and the man with the bowler hat and the umbrella were not connected.

He slept well, and was called just after seven-thirty by Jolly, with the post and the papers.

"Is there anything in the headlines?" Rollison asked.

"Nothing of great importance, sir," said Jolly. "I have opened the post."

"Thanks," said Rollison. "All right."

He looked through the *Gazette*, drank a cup of tea, and took the letters from the envelopes which Jolly had slit at the top. There were seven; the first two were notes from friends, little things of no account. The third was a bill, the fourth from an Aunt.

The writing on the fifth was familiar. It was always pleasant to hear from Diana, who had once imagined that he had broken her heart, and was now married and with three children—'like Hilda,' he thought, suddenly bleak.

Diana's sprawling writing was easy to read:

"Dear Rolly,

I suppose you are still alive? Do you know that I've written three times without so much as a post card in return? But I'll forgive you, I know how busy you must be"—Rollison grimaced—*"and as a matter of fact I've had my hands full, Peter's had measles and Janet's had mumps, I don't know which is the worst. As for help these days, its hopeless.*

"Don't scowl! I know you think the world is a terrible mess, and you have high-falutin' ideas about making it a better place, and, of course, I agree with you, although it's not easy to see how it will work. People are selfish, you know.

"By the way, do you know a man named Guy? A funny little fellow who talks with a lisp? He called

23

here the other day and asked for you—why he thought you might be here I don't know. He said he owed you something or other—a very old debt, seven years old—and he was anxious to find you to repay it. He was rather wearying. I gave him your London address, but told him you were probably abroad— are you, by the way?"

Rollison stopped reading, and looked out of the window to see the roofs of the other houses reflecting the morning sun; his eyes were bleak. He re-read that paragraph; he did not know a man named Guy, but it's significance was all too clear. He finished the letter, which was filled with little anecdotes about the children, and then read the postscript.

"Rolly, I know its silly, but that little man, Guy, has rather got on my mind. There was something I didn't like about him, almost—don't laugh!—sinister. Do write and set my mind at rest."

Rollison put the letter aside, and looked without interest at the remaining letters—both of which had been left unsealed. He opened them mechanically; the first was a bill, the second a newspaper cutting which was folded, and yellow at the corners. He smoothed it out, his heart beating faster when he saw that it was a cutting of what he had read from the old *Gazette. There was nothing else*; just the part that he had selected so as to recall the way Charmion had looked across the court-room at him, motionless yet menacing.

Rollison lay back for a few minutes, smoking a cigarette. Then he looked at Diana's letter again, at the cutting, and thought of Fifi and Joe, of Hilda, the bowler-hatted man and Georgina's story. His full well-shaped lips curved in a slow smile which widened until it showed his large, white teeth.

Then in a loud voice he cried:

"Jolly! *Jolly!*"

Only a slight pause followed before Jolly appeared.

"Jolly, it's on!" said Rollison, and he sounded almost gay. "Charmion's on the trail. After him, Jolly! Run my bath, try to get Grice again, then get Miss Georgina Scott on the other line and ask her if she can lunch with me. If she can't, coffee at eleven. If she's engaged for that, tell her that if she leaves the house before I see her this morning I'll never speak to her again." He tied the cord of his dressing-gown about him and breezed into the bathroom to shave.

He had lathered one side of his face when Jolly said that Grice was on the telephone. Rollison went into his study, and picked up the receiver.

"Now what's got you up so early?" demanded Grice, who sounded sour. "I haven't had three hours' sleep."

"Sorry, old chap, but I must see you this morning."

"It will have to be after twelve," said Grice. "I'm due at Marlborough Street."

"Is it important?"

"Important enough," said Grice. "What's worrying you, Rolly? I'm really so full up that—"

"Charmion," said Rollison, as if the name was an *Open Sesame*. He was mildly disappointed when Grice seemed unimpressed.

"Well, what about him?"

"That's what I want to tell you about, but not over the telephone," said Rollison. "Shall we say twelve-fifteen?"

"All right," said Grice, and rang off.

Rollison finished shaving, and was in his bath when Jolly said that Miss Scott would not be free for lunch, but would be happy to meet Mr. Rollison at eleven o'clock, at the Kettledrum, but that she would only have a quarter of an hour to spare. Rollison enjoyed his breakfast and, immediately afterwards, ran through the reports of the Charmion case again. They affected him very differently from the night before; the only thing that made him sober up was thought of the attack upon Hilda Brent. He telephoned the Yard, this time asking for Sergeant

Wilcox, whom he knew was liaison officer between the Yard and the Division which covered Hilda's district.

Wilcox recalled the case, he said; a nasty business, but not isolated. There were fewer of them in London than in other parts of the country. No, the men responsible had not been caught; it was not certain whether they had been in uniform or not.

Rollison said, "Thanks," and replaced the receiver, going into the kitchen, where Jolly was busy.

"Would you remember Charmion if you saw him again?"

"I certainly would, sir!"

"Good. Look for him!" Rollison waved a hand, airily. "I don't know where you'll find him, but he might be in London. Inquire, pry, prod. The magic word is Charmion. You've enough imagination to find a good reason for looking for him, haven't you?"

"I think so, sir," said Jolly, cautiously.

"Good!" said Rollison, smiling widely. "The needle in the haystack was no harder a quest than this. I know! The thing is, we aren't going to sit back here and wait for it; the hunt's up. You'd better 'phone me here or at the Carillon if there is anything of interest—oh, I'll be at the Yard from twelve-fifteen onward, and Grice will probably lunch with me. All right?"

"Yes, sir," said Jolly.

He did not relish it; Rollison knew that, knew also that at the back of his own mind he was as apprehensive as Jolly. Only his reluctance to sit back and wait for Charmion to make the first attack compelled him to go out and look for trouble.

He was ready before Jolly, and at a quarter to eleven walked towards the Kettledrum, a small coffee-house off Piccadilly which had flourished since the war; it had one entrance in Old Bond Street, where its popularity as a rendezvous increased every day.

Georgina was waiting.

She wore a tailor-made suit of light green sharkskin, with a green hat to match; the trimmings were the colour of her lovely auburn hair. Usually her eyes were glowing, for she was full of life and always in a hurry. As Rollison approached her, however, she was sitting at a small corner table and staring at a card—a menu card, Rollison thought at first. In fact it was an ordinary post card. As Rollison reached her, she looked up; she was pale.

"Hallo, 'Gina," he said. "You look worried."

"We-ell," said Georgina, "I am, rather. Such a queer thing happened, Rolly. Just as I was coming in a man pushed against me—it was rather unpleasant. I found afterwards that he'd tucked this card into my coat—" She put her hand between two of the buttons of the coat, to make clear what she meant. "He was a funny little man, but I didn't like the way he said: 'Give this to Rollison.' I mean, Rolly, how could he know that I was meeting you? And what does 'Charmion' mean?"

Rollison managed to keep a sober face.

"It's a name for charming people," he said, lightly. "I think you've been dreaming dreams, 'Gina. Let's sit down." He pulled a chair out for her, and beckoned to a waitress, trying not to show exceptional interest in the card she held lightly. She sat down, slowly, and put the card in front of her; the side which was upwards was quite blank.

Normally, she would have said indignantly that she had not been dreaming; now much of her natural vivacity seemed to have been drained away. Rollison ordered coffee, and picked up the card, saying:

"Are you sure he said you were to give it to me? And where did you get the name Charmion?"

"Of course I'm sure!" said Georgina. "And I *don't* go about day-dreaming, Rolly! It's so queer. The name—I read it on the card."

He turned the card, and then looked up at her.

"'Gina," he said, gently, "what kind of game is this? There's nothing written here at all."

CHAPTER IV

NO EVIDENCE AT ALL

Georgina stared at him, her eyes gradually losing their dullness, and sparkling with a sudden resentment which was much more natural.

"I know there isn't, but there was! It faded in front of my eyes. There was one word—Charmion. It was in green ink, and I thought there was something the matter with my eyes when it began to grow faint. Then you arrived, and I looked round—and the next time I glanced at the card there was nothing. Rolly, is this a practical joke?" She began to smile, and dimples appeared, unexpectedly. "Oh, you idiot! You've been fooling me!"

Rollison shook his head.

"You have!" she insisted, and then the coffee arrived, and she began to pour it out, her eyes brimming over with humour. "What a priceless ass you are, Rolly! Of course, disappearing ink! I *am* a fool to have let it upset me. I don't know why it did, except—he was rather a beast, and it was a shock to have the card pushed at me. He—" She narrowed her eyes and held the coffee-pot suspended over a cup. "Rolly, what are you looking like that for?"

He was staring past her, through the window.

A man moved on. Rollison caught sight of him only for a moment, but it was long enough to see the wavy hair, the sardonic smile on the full lips, and almost feminine beauty. It was Charmion, as he had seen him seven years before. Time might have stood still during those years, for the man, spending the prison-life like a Rip Van Winkle, and resuming precisely where he had left off.

Rollison knew that it would be useless for him to go

outside to try to catch up with the man, and he lit a cigarette. Georgina brushed a wave of hair back from the side of her face and handed him his cup.

"What *is* the matter?" she demanded. "You look as if you'd seen a ghost."

"Ah," said Rollison, relaxing. "Yes, one might say a ghost. 'Gina, do you remember talking to me on the telephone last night?"

"Of course, I do."

"The man you saw at the Savoy with Teddy—it was Teddy Marchant, wasn't it?"

"Yes. He was so anxious I should tell you."

"I'm glad he was. Now tell me if I'm describing the man who mentioned my name."

He gave her a vivid pen-picture of Charmion—just as the man had been in the photograph and at the window. As he spoke he knew that two things were grievously wrong. In the first place, it was not natural that Charmion should have altered so little, and in any case his hair would not be long if he had just come out of jail. In the second place, Charmion would not have been able to guess that he was coming here to meet Georgina. The fact that the appointment had been known was alarming; Rollison fought a losing battle against believing it.

Georgina widened her lovely eyes and said:

"What *are* you talking about, Rolly? He was nothing like that at all! I told you—or did I forget?—that he had closecropped hair. Like a convict's. That was why Teddy was so anxious that I should tell you about it; he seemed to think—but, of course, you *do* send men to prison, don't you?"

Rollison gulped.

"I help them to get there at times," he admitted. "*Nothing* like my description, you say?"

"Nothing at all like it. But then, I only caught just a glimpse of him, and he had his eyes half-closed. He was rather a peculiar-looking man in some ways—he didn't look quite natural. His face was pale—unhealthy, as if he'd been living underground for a long time."

"What about his voice?"

"There wasn't anything very unusual about it," said Georgina; "it was just a voice. Rolly, are you sure you haven't been pulling my leg?"

"No tricks from me," said Rollison. "On me, perhaps. How many people have you told that you were coming to meet me here this morning?"

"Why, no one."

"Now, come," reproved Rollison. "Didn't you mention it to a single soul? Just as an item of gossip, or as a reason why you simply *had* to leave them with hardly a word?"

"Brute!" exclaimed Georgina. "You're laughing at me. I'm all mixed up, Rolly, and I'm sure it's only because of the nasty look in that little man's eyes. I told Mother, of course. I might have just happened to mention in passing to one or two people. I've been to the Committee office in Lewis Street, and there are always dozens there. We had a lot to do, and there was rather a strained atmosphere when I said I absolutely had to come out, but your man sounded so serious on the 'phone that I daren't let you down. And my maid, of course, she knew—she made a note on the pad for me as soon as I'd finished on the telephone. I was just going to have a bath. And I remember now, I met Peggy Bliss—you know Peggy, don't you?—and I told her."

"Just in passing," murmured Rollison, faintly.

"That's right," said Georgina, earnestly. "She was coming out of a shop, and we stopped for a moment. I—Rolly!"

"Go on," he said, resignedly.

"Do you know, I could swear I saw that funny little man outside the shop where I met Peggy. He was standing and looking in the window—it was a display of lingerie, some men are like that. He looked just the type, too. Of course, I might be wrong, but I'm almost sure. Anyway, it doesn't matter, does it? Do you know, I feel much better now that we've been able to talk it over. Shall I keep the card, or will you?"

"I'd like to," said Rollison, taking it and slipping it into his pocket. "Now before you go—"

"But I absolutely *must* fly, Rolly! You've no idea the number of black looks I received when I came out, they're always like that these days. I don't know why they should be; after all, it's only voluntary work and I put absolutely *hours* in."

"If you have to stay here an hour more," said Rollison grimly, "you'll describe the funny little man."

"Isn't that a good enough description? Funny-looking? I don't remember anything about him, except that he had rather beady brown eyes, and funny little bushy eyebrows; you know how some people's grow, you'd think they'd pluck them, or cut them, or something. And he was just like a parrot—that's funny, he talked like one, too!"

"Oh," said Rollison. "He talked like a parrot?"

"Yes," went on Georgina serenely. "He couldn't quite form his words properly, he had a lisp. Well, not exactly a lisp, but something like that, and he couldn't really roll his 'r's.' I mean, he made it sound more like 'Wollison.' No. '*Wollithon*,' so I suppose he couldn't sound his esses, either, and that means he did have a lisp, doesn't it?"

Rollison agreed that it did.

When she had gone he stood by himself opposite Hatchards. But though he was looking across the road, he saw neither the windows of the bookshop nor the people passing by; he did not even reflect upon the number of obvious foreigners.

A little man, named Guy, and talking with a lisp, had called on Diana in Hertfordshire; surely Georgina's little man was the same?

He took a taxi to Marlborough Street, stopped at the Police Court, asking the first sergeant he saw whether the Court was still sitting; it was, and the sergeant also told him that Superintendent Grice was there.

"You're not interested in this case, Mr. Rollison, are you?" asked the sergeant.

"Crime passes me by these days," smiled Rollison.

31

"Oh, yes?" said the sergeant, sceptically. "Once it's in the blood like it's in yours, Mr. Rollison, you can't get it out! And the case that Superintendent Grice is on this morning—well, it was the kind of thing that would have interested you a lot in the old days."

"Why, what is it?"

"Snow," said the sergeant succinctly. "Cocaine, Mr. Rollison. There's a lot of the stuff about these days. It's wicked, isn't it? Mostly women, too. It's natural they like a little excitement, I suppose, to take themselves out of it, but if you was to ask me, if they went in for less excitement and set about living properly, they'd—"

He broke off, and hurried away, for the door of the courtroom opened and two or three detectives walked out, footsteps echoing in the barely-furnished passage. Then the general public filtered out, and through the open door Rollison could see the prisoner going into a room opposite. Grice was with him.

Rollison was looking hard at the Superintendent when a deep voice spoke at his side.

"Hallo, hallo, if it isn't the Toff! Are you in this case, Rolly?"

Rollison gazed, not with favour, upon a jovial-looking, red-faced man who had a dilapidated trilby upon the back of his head and was wearing a badly-soiled macintosh. This worthy was in the act of lighting a cigarette; he offered one from a battered packet to Rollison, who accepted, lit up and said:

"I am not."

"Emphatic negative means an affirmative, or am I wrong?" demanded the other. "Seriously, old man, have you got anything? These Police Court jobs are the very devil these days, hardly worth reporting, but you never know what you might miss. This is just another snow case, except"—a pair of large, shrewd eyes narrowed—"Oh-*ho*! I thought Grice was taking more interest than he usually does. Grice—and then you. Now come on, let's have the lowdown. If I could get a really good break it would help a lot, Rolly. The Press is a dog's life these days, unless you're on the political or military side."

"The emphatic negative meant 'no'," Rollison assured him easily. "I'm not in it, Mike. I want to see Grice before I leave Town again, and they told me I'd find him here."

"Just for old time's sake?" grinned Mike, sceptically.

"No," said Rollison. "A friend of mine had a nasty time in Mile End a few days ago, and I want to find out who was behind it." He looked hopeful. "Do you know the case I mean?"

He knew that he had to give Mike Anderson, of the *Echo*, a reasonable explanation of waiting to see Grice, or he would be in danger of being dogged by a reporter who was reputed to have a nose for news and who was certainly persistent. At the same time, it was possible that Anderson would know something of the attack on Hilda Brent. The last thing he wanted was to arouse Anderson's curiosity too much.

Anderson raised an eyebrow.

"There are lots of nasty affairs in the Mile End, Rolly. You ought to know—it's your beat."

"Ye-es," said Rollison. "I haven't been there much lately." His feeling of disquiet increased; he was always sensitive to trouble east of Aldgate.

Anderson shrugged.

"More's the pity! What's your particular worry?"

"A woman named Hilda Brent," said Rollison, "she was attacked and beaten up."

"Nothing worse?"

"No."

"We just haven't got much room for that stuff these days," said Anderson, "but you might find something in the local rag—I don't need to tell you which it is. I must get going. I'll do a column-and-a-half on this morning's stuff and it'll be cut to about four inches."

He nodded and went out. Soon Grice came hurrying out with an inspector and a sergeant. He stopped at sight of Rollison, spoke to the inspector in an aside, and then approached Rollison as the inspector and the sergeant went out.

Grice was a lean, spare man, dressed in brown; he had brown eyes which had been called soulful, although Rollison did not subscribe to that description; they were watchful eyes which missed very little. Not particularly good-looking, the Superintendent had a remarkably fine complexion; it was almost transparent, and the skin was stretched taut over his pointed nose, making him look thinner than he was.

He shook hands and smiled a little crookedly.

"So you couldn't wait until I was at the office?"

"Must you go back to the office, or can you have lunch with me?"

"Thanks, I will," said Grice.

"Good—we'll take a cab." Rollison directed the driver to the Carillon, then sat back beside Grice, who stretched his long legs.

"I don't think I should have told you that Charmion was out," he said. "You've been imagining that he's busy, I suppose?"

Rollison said: "Why suppose anything of the kind?"

"Need we fence?" asked Grice. "One thing's certain, Rolly. It isn't Charmion. He's not been out long enough. None of his one-time friends are in it, and I don't think any of them are very interested in Charmion himself. No, it's something new this time. I suppose I'll have to spend the whole of the next two hours convincing you, but you're an astonishing fellow—how did you know what was afoot?"

"Oh," said Rollison, carefully, "these things get around." The Superintendent's words had made it abundantly clear that there was some trouble on similar lines to that for which Charmion had been sentenced.

If he declared that he had no idea of what Grice was talking about probably Grice would give him no information. Yet he wanted to know what it was all about; he convinced himself that it was necessary for him to know.

34

The taxi stopped outside the Carillon; Rollison climbed out and was paying the driver off while Grice slammed the door when a man on a bicycle passed the cab and tossed something in the air. It was small and round, and it caught Rollison unawares, striking him on the temple as he heard the cabby's exclamation and another, urgent and alarmed, from Grice.

CHAPTER V

NOT LETHAL

Liquid splashed against the Toff's temple and ran down his cheek and his neck between his skin and the collar. The impact of the missile was light; it just burst against him and then sagged down, the liquid dripping from it.

Grice gripped Rollison's arm and peered at his streaming eyes. Rollison opened them quickly and blinked the stuff away. He shook the liquid from his face as best he could, then dabbed himself with a handkerchief. A little had trickled into his mouth.

"I think it's water."

"Water!" exclaimed Grice.

"Yes. Did I pay you, cabby?"

"Er—yessir, thank you." Startled eyes surveyed Rollison's dripping face, and then, from force of habit, the driver drove off.

Rollison led the way into the Club, signed Grice in, and hurried down to the cloakroom. Neither man spoke. Grice had retrieved the sodden cloth, which had been wrapped outside a paper bag in turn containing the water. It was a childish contraption, a booby-trap without subtlety.

"We'd better be sure it is water," said Grice.

"Oh, it is," said Rollison, drying his face in front of the mirror. "I would have known by now if it had been anything else. You might call it a weapon, but it wasn't lethal. In fact"—he threw the towel into a basket and took another to rub his collar—"it's in keeping with all that's happened. Someone has decided that a war of nerves is going to yield results."

"But, confound it!" exclaimed Grice, who rarely used even the mildest of expletives, and because of which was regarded with some awe by his subordinates and was not wholly trusted by his equals. "Who on earth would want to throw water over you? Where's the sense in it?"

"Tactics," said Rollison, "*vide* Charmion."

Grice said: "There isn't the slightest evidence that Charmion is behind this business, and you ought to know that from the beginning. I know it's remarkably like the Charmion affair—"

"Another League of Physical Beauty?" asked Rollison.

"You could call it that."

"A galaxy of neurotic talent?"

"Neurotic, yes," said Grice. "Some evidence of drugs —but there's no need to tell you that."

"Oh, there's ample need to tell me everything," said Rollison. "I think I'm all right now; let's go upstairs, or the dining-room will be crowded out." He led the way to the first floor, but there was plenty of room and they were able to get a table for two, near a window and a serving-trolley, so that no one would overhear them easily. They ordered soup and steak pie, Rollison a tankard of beer and Grice grapefruit squash.

"Bill," said Rollison, as the waitress went away, "I've a confession to make." He smiled into Grice's eyes and broke a roll. "I knew nothing at all about your new League, or whatever you're calling it, until five minutes ago."

Grice said with acerbity:

"There's no need to—"

"It's gospel truth."

"But Charmion—"

"Yes, I'm worried about Charmion and I think he's up to tricks, but I hadn't any idea that he's mixed up with your current trouble. I know you can't believe it, but facts are facts!" Rollison ate a piece of bread. "The Scarlet Pimpernel has nothing on him! He looks in here, he sends messages there, he writes in invisible ink, he approaches me through friends and acquaintances, and he throws water over me. Ah, beer!" He raised a tankard brought to the table and Grice sipped cautiously at his grapefruit squash. "Confusion to Charmion!" he said. "Would it help if I told you all of it?"

"Yes," said Grice, emphatically.

Rollison told the story, filling in the outline which he had already given, and bringing it up to date. They had finished the soup by the time he reached the end, and the waitress was at Rollison's elbow with the entree. When she had gone, Grice put both elbows on the table and, with steam from vegetables rising in his face, said slowly:

"That's absolutely everything?"

"I haven't another particle of information," said Rollison. "I can only guess that Charmion is trying to goad me into some great folly." He smiled. "The only really ugly part about it is Hilda Brent's affair. That's not nice. You don't remember the report, I suppose?"

"Vaguely," said Grice. "There have been similar attacks, of course. They're difficult to trace, but we've prevented them from getting too numerous. Y'know, Rollison"—he started to eat—"I find it hard to believe that the attack on the girl was made so that you would hear of it and connect it with Charmion. It sounds too fantastic."

"Charmion is, and always will be, fantastic," said Rollison. "You didn't know him personally, did you? No. A pity; you might have assessed him accurately. No one at the Yard did, and some were half-inclined to believe that he was innocent. The expression often used is personal magnetism! Grice, Charmion first of all made sure that a casual remark would be passed on to me, to make me bring him to mind, and he guessed that my first reaction would be to find out what was happening to Hilda—the chief witness for the prosecution on the drug case. He didn't do it himself, of course; it started a long time before he was released, so he made the arrangements with someone working for him outside. And this someone might be your man, whom it won't be easy to connect with Charmion." He smiled. "Feeling any happier than you were?"

"I am not," said Grice. "Rolly, if anyone else had told me this I would have called it a fairy story and left it at that."

"Charmion's a fairy-story name," murmured Rollison.

"As it is—what can I do about it?"

"You can check up on all that's happened to Hilda and her children; there's a chance of getting results that way. The thing is, I can spare the time just now. I don't like Charmion, and I think he is preparing a devil's brew in which I'm one of the most potent ingredients. You should know that I won't find it easy to remain idle."

"I can't blame you. Just what's in your mind?"

Rollison shrugged.

"Charmion would brood over this while in jail and be prepared to wait and work for revenge—but not revenge alone. He may have marked me down—or Hilda, or any-one who had a part in his fall, but we should be inciden-tal. Notable incidents, perhaps, but not the beginning and the end of his ambitions. He might"—Rollison eyed Grice steadily—"conceivably have some grandiose no-tion of getting revenge on society, the system which sent him to seven years of okum-picking and stone-breaking. A lot of people are bitter after seven years on the moor."

"Aren't you putting it a bit extravagantly?"

"I don't think so," said Rollison, soberly. "If I haven't misjudged him, Charmion will be burning with a hatred which will get hotter every day. He's starting mildly, but he has a long-term plan. Your bother may be part of it—we'll see. As for me—" he smiled crookedly—"I am going to fall for the bait. Charmion wants me to go after him, and I'm going. As I said, I think you should know."

Grice eyed him without speaking.

"Because," continued Rollison, "Charmion is going to try to lead me up the garden with a large hole at the bot-tom of it, filled with the necessary spikes and sharp knives. That's an allegory," he added, brightly. "I mean—"

"You mean that you think he's going to try to make you fall foul of the law?" suggested Grice, slowly.

"Now who could have put it neater than that?" de-manded Rollison. "Yes, that will be Charmion's most likely plan of campaign. I sent him away, he'll try to send me away. That won't be all, there'll be something else. How's your thinking cap these days?"

Grice shrugged. "It works, sometimes."

"I've an uncomfortable feeling that it will have to work at double pressure," said Rollison, "but that will settle itself. Now, what about your own pet problem?"

Grice smiled. "Now that you've wormed most of it out of me, you may as well know the rest."

The waitress came up and offered them a choice of three equally appetising sweets, over which decision Rollison took much time. He was finding it difficult to be really interested in what Grice had to say—it would matter only if it could be traced to Charmion.

"I'm working on patchwork evidence, Rolly. I thought I had something this morning, but it flopped. There was a girl on a drug-addict charge. Not serious—she's only been toying with it, and a sharp lesson will probably put her right. We shall watch her, of course. The significant thing—as I thought at first—is that she's a member of a little club in Port Street."

"Ah!" exclaimed Rollison.

"Why that exclamation?" demanded Grice.

"The headquarters of Charmion's League was in Port Street," Rollison said, "but, of course, that's only coincidence. Yes?"

"It's an innocent-seeming place," Grice told him. "Physical training as much as anything else—gymnastics, Turkish baths. It's run by the people who run a dancing club in Littleton Place. The dancing club is very proper, to all outward appearances. Ballroom dancing, a good tutor, lessons in etiquette—the usual incubator for social aspirants."

Rollison frowned. "In the fifth year of this war?"

"Of course, that's the snag," said Grice. "It's hard to believe that it's all it seems. It isn't, either! There's a higher price club, where the dancing is considerably less formal, probably a bit orgiastic—but there's nothing we can really do about it. I think there may be a higher echelon still, but I can't be sure. The thing is, Rolly, one or two of the members of both clubs have started taking drugs. We haven't been able to find where they get the stuff. I'd hoped this morning that the girl would be able to name the source of supply, but her story petered out. The usual man in the park, or at a street corner, a package of snow in exchange for notes. The only thing we did get this time was a description of the man—the exchange took place in daylight, which was a slip-up. We might get some results from it."

It was the same old story; there seemed no end to the folly of sensation-craving youth. He felt a little bitter, for he as well as the police had been fighting against it for many years, but as soon as one loophole was closed up another opened. In his mind, also, was thought of Hilda Brent, Georgina and Diana—three people less alike it would be hard to find; he wished he could find the true common denominator.

Grice went on:

"It was quite a vivid description, too. The man was a little fellow, with a hooked nose, bushy eyebrows, and a lisp. Of course, the lisp could have been assumed, but—" Grice paused because of the change of expression on Rollison's face. "*Now* what's the matter?"

Rollison said, softly: "And you think there's no connection with Charmion? Bill! that's my man. *The* man! The writer in invisible ink, the man who called himself Guy. We're really on the move!"

CHAPTER VI

OF THE LITTLE MAN
NAMED GUY

There was little they could do, although Grice left the Club in a troubled frame of mind while Rollison, happy at the thought that the police now had reason to search for Guy, and convinced that Guy would lead to Charmion, was less uneasy, if still concerned lest Charmion should prepare a trap for him which he could not avoid, one to put him on the wrong side of the law. None other was likely.

Rollison telephoned the flat from the Club, but there was no reply; apparently Jolly was still out on his quest. Then he rang Diana, who was delighted to hear from him.

"Does this mean we are going to see something of you? Do try to come down, Rolly. George is home for a week."

"I will try," Rollison assured her, "but this is just to set your mind at rest—I hope," he added, cautiously.

"You mean about that man named Guy?" asked Diana. "He made quite an impression on you, didn't he?"

"Yes, he did, rather. I don't know why, but—well, if you know him, that's all right."

"I remember him," said Rollison, mendaciously. "Di, if he should turn up again, I want you to try to telephone a message to me while he's there. Don't make it obvious, but try. Will you?"

Diana was silent for so long that Rollison said sharply: "Are you there?"

"Ye-es," said Diana, heavily. "So it does mean trouble?"

"No, not trouble, but—"

"You needn't try to be reassuring," said Diana. "I suspected it from the first; that's why I wrote to you. There was something really evil about him. I can't explain it, but—oh, well, I suppose nothing will ever change you."

"Oh, I'm all right," said Rollison, and jollied her. "It's not serious."

"I don't believe a word you say," Diana declared, roundly. She sounded very sober. "I'll ring through if he does come, Rolly, I promise you that. You won't be coming up, then?"

"Just as soon as I can I'll see you," Rollison promised.

He rang off, and was very thoughtful as he went to the smoking-room and sat down, stretching his legs and looking through the window into St. James's Park. There were comparatively few members in the room, and the only sound was of heavy breathing, the rustle of papers and the occasional murmur of conversation. None of those things disturbed his reverie, centred upon the little man named Guy.

"Or calling himself Guy," he mused aloud.

A man who could create such an impression on so healthy-minded a person as Diana, who could startle and disturb so light-hearted a creature as Georgina, was no ordinary fellow. To Rollison, it seemed that Guy had made one major mistake—that of allowing himself to be seen when he had peddled snow. Yet this affair was developing so swiftly and proving itself so well organized that it was difficult to believe that it had been a mistake. It was very rare for dope-pushers to allow themselves to be seen distinctly enough for clear identification, yet this man had made a marked impression on the girl whom Grice had charged at Marlborough Street.

A voice disturbed his reverie.

"Mr. Rollison, please! Mr. Rollison!"

Rollison looked round, raising a hand. A call-boy came towards him with a slip of paper, saying: "Telephone, sir."

"Thanks," Rollison glanced down at the message and frowned, for it was brief and unexpected, and it introduced a new element of urgency into the situation. It

43

took him so much by surprise and impressed him more, because it was from Jolly.

"If at all possible, please return at once."

Rollison left the Club, finding a taxi outside and telling the man to hurry to Gresham Terrace. Sitting back in the cab he was deep in thought.

Jolly might have sent the message, but someone else could have put the call through and given his name as Jolly; this might be another step in the campaign to harass and confuse him. He paid the driver and turned towards the front door, his lips pursed, his expression suggesting that he was in no way perturbed, yet he contrived to look up at the window of his flat; he thought he saw the curtain move, but could not be sure. He put his right hand deep into his trousers pocket, and wished that he carried a gun.

He whistled as he reached the second-floor landing and inserted a key in the lock. Opening the door, he pushed it away from him and stepped swiftly to one side.

Jolly's voice greeted him, quietly.

"Is that you, sir?"

"Oh," said Rollison, almost disappointed. "Yes." He widened the door and stepped through, but Jolly was not in the little hall. There was a movement in the study, and Rollison stepped towards its open door.

He stopped on the threshold.

Jolly stood in front of his desk, upon which was an incredible thing—a stuffed effigy of ludicrous appearance, with a mask-like face which might have been that of a parrot rather than a man. Yet the life-like impression was startling. There was the little beaked nose and the bushy eyebrows, an incredibly sly and cunning look in beady, brown eyes—artificial eyes, not buttons made to serve.

The effigy was complete from the waist upwards; the chest, with a coat fastened about it, was puffed out, a green tie and a blue collar added a touch of colour that made it more grotesque.

Jolly said: "I thought I'd better send for you at once, sir."

"Ye-es," said Rollison, tipping his hat back. "A present from Charmion, I suppose? Ingenious-looking thing, isn't it? We're rated high, Jolly." He approached the bust. "Not a bad piece of sculpture, either. Was this just how you found it?"

"Exactly like this, sir. I've discovered that several things are missing, though."

"Such as?" Rollison asked, sharply.

"The phials of cocaine which you kept as souvenirs of the Charmion case," said Jolly, "and the files on Charmion. His photograph has gone and all the press-cuttings. You left them on the desk, if you remember, sir."

"I do," admitted Rollison. "All gone, and this in their place. Clever, these people."

"I *was* startled, sir," said Jolly. "I'm sorry that I did not wait to speak to you in person, but I was just a little apprehensive—I imagined that I heard a movement in the kitchen, and considered it wise to get word to you immediately before making a search. I"—Jolly looked regretful—"I think I was mistaken. I could find no trace of anyone. In fact, if it were not for this room, there would be no sign of felonious entry whatsoever."

"Hum," said Rollison, and murmured aloud: "Thinking caps, decidedly."

"I beg your pardon, sir?"

"Thinking caps," said Rollison. "I was discussing them with Grice. It makes us think. What does it make us think? Does it make us think what we should or what someone else would like us to?" He contemplated the bust for some seconds, then shot a sidelong glance towards Jolly. "Am I talking drivel?"

"I think you're a little preoccupied," said Jolly, tactfully.

"Yes. Have you touched the thing yet?"

"No, sir. I thought it wiser to leave it severely alone." He eyed the thing with extreme suspicion.

"So do I," said Rollison, "but I can't. Someone threw some water over me outside the Club," he added, dreamily. "For a second or two I was sure it was a Mills bomb, and expected to wake up in the next world. A booby-trap of an innocuous nature, of course. This is Number 2. Unfortunately, it might not be so harmless as the first. Go and make me some tea, Jolly, will you?"

"I'd rather stay here, sir," said Jolly. "I presume you propose to dismantle it now?"

"We'll have to start, one day. We can't keep it in the flat thinking it might go off, and we can't put the job on to bomb-disposal. I'll do this by myself," he added. "You make some tea." He smiled, but made it clear that he was determined. So Jolly left the room reluctantly. Rollison, conscious of the uncomfortably fast beating of his heart, drew nearer the effigy.

Gingerly, he undid one of the coat buttons; the coat sagged, but nothing else happened. He tried the second and the third, with the same result. But there was a waist-coat beneath, and with each button Rollison felt a tension which increased, although he was absorbed in the task. He did not deceive himself; the thing might well be an infernal machine, set to go off at the slightest touch on the right place, and as such it would be in keeping with Charmion's particular sense of humour.

He took the coat off when the waistcoat was unbuttoned, then worked at the collar and tie. All the time the beady eyes stared at him, as if they were carrying a message of evil, a threat, a menace which made the room seem warm and made the Toff's hands moist.

He had stripped the thing down to the stuffed canvas carcass when Jolly came in, carrying a tea-tray. He put the tray on a small table and contemplated Rollison thoughtfully.

"Shall I pour out, sir?"

"Yes," said Rollison, preoccupied. "There's only the face now, you see. A good mask, made by an expert. Could it be Guy's real mistake? He—Jolly!"

"Yes, sir?"

"Guy!" repeated Rollison, staring wide-eyed at his man. "Guy, of course! A stuffed effigy representing the notorious Guy Fawkes—no, I'm not rambling, but it's a superb touch. The name, the effigy—Jolly, I admire these beggars!"

"One might almost think they were endeavouring to make a guy out of you, mightn't one?" said Jolly, impassively. "Strong or weak, sir?"

"Strong," said Rollison, eyeing his man suspiciously. "Is that what you think?"

"What, sir?" asked Jolly, pouring the tea.

"That they're making a convincing guy out of me?"

"Good gracious, no, sir!" Jolly looked embarrassed but contrived to convey a slight reproach in his glance. "That was the last thing in my mind, but they may *think* that is what they're doing. Many people have misjudged you in the past, and I see no reason why Charmion should judge you any better than the others. I have been thinking, as a matter of fact, that we may be crediting Charmion with more resourcefulness than he possesses," continued Jolly. "After all, he is just a man, an ordinary human being, with his limitations made greater by his incarceration during the past seven years. I am wondering if—"

"Stop it!" said Rollison, sharply. "You don't think anything of the kind."

"No, sir," said Jolly, meekly.

"What are you driving at? And have some tea yourself."

"Thank you, sir, but I had a cup immediately after lunch. I don't know that I am driving at anything in particular," continued Jolly, his lined face set in sober concentration. "I was really disturbed when I first heard you say that Charmion was free, but I have wondered since whether we have not over-estimated his powers."

"You think he's suffering from advanced senile decay? He goes to the trouble of breaking in here and having this thing planted on us, just for fun? He thinks it will amuse me, perhaps?"

"No, sir," said Jolly, "but—"

"Go on."

"We have no real assurance that Charmion sent that

here, have we?" He looked benignly upon Rollison. "I feel sure that you have perceived that obvious fact."

Rollison sipped his tea, eyeing Jolly over the top of the cup.

"So you're beginning to wonder whether it is Charmion, are you? No one else would have a mind quite like this, they would miss somewhere."

"Precisely, sir," said Jolly, "a qualification."

"And yet," continued Rollison, as if there had been no interruption, "would Charmion draw attention to himself quite so deliberately? The first moves were in keeping, so they were all right. But the theft of his press-cuttings and his photographs, the disappearance of the cocaine—hum, yes. Too direct, you think?"

"I'm beginning to, yes."

"Someone—let's call him Guy—thinks it would be a help if he were to make it appear that Charmion was on the trail," mused Rollison. "There's one thing we forget. Charmion has a strong reason for wanting to work upon my nerves. Has Guy? Has anyone else?"

"That is a point I had not considered," admitted Jolly, frowning. "It's most confusing, but—"

"We'd better finish with our Guy," said Rollison. "Pour me another cup, will you?"

He turned to the effigy and, very gently, removed the grey wig. Jolly seemed indifferent to the operation, but Rollison was intent, wondering if, at the last moment, the trap might be sprung. As he worked, his hands quite steady but his heart beating fast, he called himself a fool for taking this chance, and then reminded himself that he could expect no one else to take it for him.

The wig lay on the desk; the bald wax head of 'Guy' was revealed, shiny, smooth, bumps even showing on the cranium.

"A phrenologist's dream," said Rollison.

He removed the head, easing it gently to and fro, finding the wire which kept it in position and pulling it upwards very carefully. He felt that if there were to be an explosion, it would come now; but he was able to insert a finger into the sawdust filling of the bust, unhook the wire, and lift the head right off.

He felt warm with persiration.

"I don't think there's any likelihood of trouble now, sir," said Jolly, more confidently. "What shall we do with it?"

"Keep it there for the time being," said Rollison, and smiled with relief and amusement. "I like it, Jolly! and we've something to work on now. A genuine expert in wax models made that face. There aren't many in the country. A wig-maker of distinction made the wig, and one of the others of his fraternity might be able to identify the manufacturer. Each will have his own peculiarity —perhaps a trade-mark. And then there are the eyes. They're perfect, Jolly, as life-like as you'll find anywhere. How many eye-makers are there left in the country? Half-a-dozen at the most; it's a craft that's dying out, swamped by mass-production."

Jolly said quickly:

"You think we may be able to trace the maker, sir?"

"Yes." Rollison began to prod gently at the eyes, which sagged inwards a little, then turned the head upside down; it was hollow, and the wax was very hard, although the surface was slightly resilient. "Genuinely empty-headed," he said, "except behind the eyes—it looks as if they've even manufactured a brain for the gentleman! Did I tell you that I saw Charmion in Old Bond Street?"

"What?" cried Jolly. "In person?"

"Charmion as he was seven years ago, obviously after taking an elixir," said Rollison. "It struck a false note then, and I know why, now. It was someone made up to look like Charmion, of course. It wasn't natural. Charmion's face and complexion always looked as if they'd been touched up by an expert, and that man I saw when I was in the Kettledrum might have come out of a stage dressing-room. You see the connection? This face, perfectly made up. A man made to look like Charmion, everything set to make me look for Charmion. I wonder if Grice—"

"I'd rather like to find out whether *I* can trace the maker of the face sir," said Jolly. "You will remember that I have mentioned my friendship with Saul Lauriston, of the Arts Club. I feel sure that he would be able to identify the maker."

"Meaning that you found no trace of Charmion this morning."

"I didn't sir, but I don't think there was ever very much hope," said Jolly. "Of course, if you prefer to ask Mr. Grice—"

He paused, hopefully. Rollison, suddenly becoming absorbed in the padding behind the eyes of the face, did not speak, but prodded at it gently with his forefinger. He felt the material sag inwards—and then, without warning, the padding broke. He heard a faint hissing sound, and saw a little cloud of vapour, and he dropped the head and backed away, coughing, his eyes feeling as if they were on fire.

CHAPTER VII

UNEXPECTED VISITOR

Rollison said, thickly:

"Blast him! It's ammonia gas."

"Am—ammonia, sir," gasped Jolly. "I—I really think you're right, sir."

They stood on either side of the hand-basin in the bathroom, bathing their eyes with sponges and looking at each other through tears, coughing all the time. They were better now but the ammonia still made their nostrils smart and gave a peculiar dryness to their lips and mouths.

Before leaving the study, Rollison had flung the window up to let out the smell, and the air in the room was clear enough when they returned, chastened and, in Rollison's case at least, feeling a little ridiculous. At the back of his mind was one disturbing fact: had there been some lethal gas behind the eyes he would have fallen for it just as easily.

Like the water, it had been a booby-trap; like the water it proved how easily he could have been injured. Had the water container been a Mills bomb, or had the ammonia been cyanide or even phosgene or its equivalent—

"Will it be all right for me to try to find out who made the head and the eyes, sir?" asked Jolly.

"Yes," said Rollison. "We'll give Grice a miss this time. You can't go out yet, you look as if you've been crying your heart out!" He smiled, but not good-humouredly. It was as if Charmion were standing near-by, laughing at him in sardonic mockery.

It *must* be Charmion.

Yet Jolly had been right to raise the query; it was too obviously Charmion. Had anyone else been involved,

Rollison would have felt sure that it was an effort to make him concentrate upon Charmion and miss the real issue.

"Apart from the head and eyes," said Jolly, "there isn't a great deal we can do."

"No," admitted Rollison. "But there might be soon. I shouldn't be at all surprised if Charmion were to walk in now and ask me how I were getting on," he added.

It was half an hour after he had identified the gas, and they were looking more normal and clearer-eyed. Jolly had made a neat parcel of the head of the effigy; he left the flat soon afterwards, leaving Rollison in a thoroughly dissatisfied frame of mind. He was jumpy, and when a car back-fired in the street he got from his chair quickly, looking down into the street but keeping close to the wall, to make sure that he could not be seen from below.

Walking sedately along the pavement on the other side of the street was a neatly-dressed man, wearing a bowler hat and carrying a furled umbrella.

Rollison turned, stepped swiftly across the room and hurried downstairs. He was quite sure that it was the man who had followed him on the previous evening; the fellow was pursing his lips as if whistling under his breath, and the slow, steady gait was exactly the same.

Rollison almost collided with a tenant of one of the lower flats, apologised hastily, and reached the street. He looked towards the Piccadilly end, where the man had been walking, but there was no sign of his quarry.

"Well, well!" said Rollison, a little vacantly.

He walked rapidly as far as the end of the road, but his man was not hiding in a doorway. He retraced his steps and reached the far corner, still without finding anyone. He walked back more leisurely, but the uncomfortable feeling of being constantly spied upon increased, making him feel even more jumpy. He whistled aloud to keep his spirits up, and when he returned to the flat lit a cigarette and stepped to the window, with no specific thought in his mind.

The man in the bowler hat was walking on the opposite side of the street!

Rollison stood quite still.

His sedate air gave the man a peculiar kind of jauntiness; his very presence was a challenge. He did not look right or left, but instead of whistling he was smiling and looking thoroughly pleased with himself.

Rollison stepped to the telephone. It had a long lead and he was able to carry it nearer the window, so that he could look out as he talked. The man in the bowler hat disappeared from his line of vision for a moment, but returned soon afterwards, just as Rollison, after dialing Scotland Yard, said quickly:

"Is Superintendent Grice there, please?"

"I'll see, sir," said the operator.

Rollison's quarry walked past the window again and then Grice came on the line, to say:

"Grice speaking."

"Send me a man," said Rollison, imploringly. "A good tailer, Grice, who will really make himself inconspicuous. Send him over to the Terrace as soon as possible, will you, and tell him to watch and follow a man in a bowler hat, with a morning coat and striped trousers and carrying a furled umbrella. Tell him—"

"What's the man been doing?" demanded Grice.

"Disappearing," said Rollison. "Every time I go after him he vanishes. It's the neatest trick I've ever seen, but your man should be proof against it, and the joker can't very well know that I'm 'phoning. Will you? For old time's sake," he added urgently. "I may be all at sea over this, Grice, but—"

"I'll send a man," said Grice.

"Good man!" said Rollison. "I'll see you later."

He replaced the receiver and approached the window more closely, but still stood on one side. His quarry walked to and fro with fine aplomb, looking neither right nor left, giving the impression that he had an appointment which he was quite sure would be kept, and that he was in no hurry.

Rollison lit a cigarette and was half-way through it when he saw another man enter Gresham Terrace, a thin, nondescript-looking fellow who walked with a slouch;

53

Rollison recognised him as Detective-Sergeant Wilson, one of the best men Grice had.

A taxi drew up outside the house; Rollison could just see it, although he was unable to see the man or woman who climbed out. He waited until the cab moved off and the bowler-hatted man continued his steady walk along the street; Wilson was nowhere in sight, but Rollison felt quite sure that he was at hand.

The front-door bell rang.

Rollison stubbed out the cigarette and went to the door, prepared to find that it was another trick; everything that happened seemed likely to prove a booby-trap, something to upset him and to quicken his tension.

When he opened the door a man of medium height, wearing a Homburg hat and a dark overcoat, stood motionlessly on the threshold.

"Good afternoon," said Rollison.

There was something vaguely familiar about the caller, although he did not recognize him. It was as if something that had happened a long time before returned to his mind, a wisp of an affair that had been important at the time but had long since passed into the limbo of forgotten things.

"Good afternoon, Rollison," said the caller. "Don't say that you have forgotten me."

"I don't recall—" began Rollison, but stopped abruptly, backing a pace, staring at the narrowed eyes, hardly able to believe what his ears told him and what his eyes began to confirm.

"I see you haven't," said the other, softly. "May I come in?"

Rollison drew back another step, held the door open, aware of a constriction at his throat.

"Ye-es. Yes, come in."

Charmion entered the flat; a very different Charmion, looking twenty years older than the man who had been in dock; his mouth had lost its ripe redness, his eyes were dull but still a peculiar brown, and his hair—as he removed his hat Rollison saw that at once—was clipped close to his head, leaving only an ugly quiff above the right eye. He spoke out of the corner of his mouth and moved forward with a queer, almost shuffling gait, as Rollison stood to one side.

Charmion stood in the middle of the small dining-alcove, hat in hand. He accepted a cigarette and a light, but did not move until Rollison said:

"Sit down, Charmion."

"Thanks." The way the one side of the man's lips moved was grotesque. He went to a chair, smoothed his coat beneath him, and sat down, but he did not relax. Rollison stood by the mantelpiece, looking down on this wreck of what had once been a man about whom women had raved, who had been lionized and almost worshipped.

Charmion's eyes were narrowed and watery, and red-rimmed. There was no expression in them, unless, thought Rollison, there was a suggestion of bitterness; but it was the bitterness of a man so devoid of feeling that it was a hardly conscious emotion.

"Well?" asked Charmion. "Are you satisfied?"

"With what?" asked Rollison.

"What you've done to me."

Rollison said, with an effort:

"I don't see it that way, Charmion."

"No-o?" The man's lips twisted, mostly on the left-hand side, evidence that he had spent so many years talking but saving himself from being heard except by his near neighbour. "You wouldn't, Rollison. When I knew what you'd done I felt like murder. If I could have got at you in court I would have killed you with my bare hands." He smiled, mirthlessly. "Oh, what is the use of talking like that? You would have bested me, of course; you were on top of the world then, probably you still are." He looked round the well-appointed recess. "You're wealthy, aren't you?"

"I have enough money," said Rollison, slowly. "Haven't you?"

"I had," said Charmion. "There was a time when I expected to become a millionaire. A millionaire!" He raised his hands and let them drop to his knees; his movements were lifeless, a robot would have looked more human. "Oh, I was rich, Rollison. I thought, once upon a time, that there would be a fortune waiting for me when I came out, and that I would be able to end my life in comfort. That was after I'd grown tired of thirsting for your blood. Do you know what a few years in Dartmoor does to a man?"

"It does various things," said Rollison, "and—"

"If you're going to tell me that it makes him regret his past, fills him with remorse, makes him determine at all costs to live a highly moral life for ever afterwards, don't waste your breath. It wastes you, Rollison; it wastes your body and your mind, it makes you into a machine, it lets you see yourself withering away, but it doesn't kill the image of what you once were. My God! There was a time when I didn't believe it possible to—"

Rollison said:

"Is this getting us anywhere?"

He wanted to stop the torrent of words which were coming faster and faster from the man's lips; they were words which reminded him of the embers of a fire, almost dead but suddenly flickering into brilliant flame. There was only a shadowy resemblance to the oratory with which Charmion had once moved thousands of people; it was grotesque.

Charmion drew a deep breath; then he coughed, took the cigarette from his lips and flung it towards the fireplace.

"I can't even taste cigarettes," he said. "I'm so used to being watched and harassed and confined in a cell that freedom frightens me, Rollison. It's a new world. Do you realise how different it is to-day from what it was when I went to Dartmoor? The war wasn't thought of then. It—I've never dreamed of anything like it. The black-out—it makes me want to scream! My nerves—" he held out his right hand; it was trembling, not violently but enough to impress Rollison, because it seemed genuine, a quiver which the man could not control. "Nerves! Me!" Charmion barked the words. "Do you remember me as I was, Rollison, or have you forgotten what I was like?"

"I haven't forgotten," said Rollison, with an effort.

"And—what do you feel towards me?"

Rollison said: "What do you expect me to feel? Pity?"

"No," said Charmion, softly, and then in a sharper voice: "No! I won't have your pity! I came to show you what you'd done to me. I hope you'll realize what it means, that you've seared my very soul, you—" he broke off, abruptly, and turned to look out of the window. "But this is madness. I'm sorry, Rollison. You see, I've had some unpleasant shocks in the past four days. I've been out for a week, but it wasn't until four days ago that I reached London. My old flat has been demolished, but I knew that. The rest—" he turned and looked into Rollison's face, his eyes glowing now; there was something that could make him feel. "There was a time when all I wanted was revenge on you and all those who had contributed towards what the pedants would call my downfall. I felt like that for two years, and then my mind became atrophied, and I had no hates, no emotions at all, only a great longing to live in comfort, to be rid of the past and the present and to get into the future. The future, Rollison, the only thing that gave me any hope, the only thing I dared think about. I had something like two hundred thousand pounds salvaged from the wreckage. I thought that would keep me in comfort and luxury for as long as I would live. You see?"

"Go on," said Rollison.

"I left it in good hands—as I thought," said Charmion, in a low-pitched voice. "Loyalty seemed to be a natural thing. I trusted them, they had the handling of the money and all my affairs. Now—"

Rollison said: "They've double-crossed you?"

"Oh, you can stand there and feel nothing and speak as if it were the most natural thing in the world!" cried Charmion. "But I trusted them, I believed in them! They've written to me, been to see me from time to time, they made me think that everything was in perfect order, that they would be waiting for me when I came

57

out. When I heard that I'd earned a year's remission I could hardly wait, it was an agony of suspense. I wrote and told them, three weeks ago, but there was no reply. Try to think what that meant, Rollison—no answer to a letter into which I'd poured my very heart! No answer—damn them! They were taken by surprise, they thought they had another year, and in that year they would have told me some plausible story about loss and misfortune, they would have pretended to be sorry. But I came out too early for them. *They've* got the money, Rollison, they've been living on it."

He stopped; he was breathing in choking gasps and his face was turning grey with the anger which burned within him. Rollison stood regarding him, expressionlessly, wondering what would follow and just how much of this was true.

At last, Charmion said:

"Well? Isn't it worth a comment?"

"Who are 'they'?" asked Rollison.

"My brother," Charmion told him. "My brother and his wife and *my* wife. You didn't know that I was married, did you? No one knew. Had the fools who came to the meetings known that I was a married man half my appeal would have been nullified. I think every one of them had some sneaking hope that they would be able to marry me!" He laughed, harshly. "Laura knew little of what I did; she wasn't very practical—or so I thought. Not practical! She's robbed me of every penny I possessed. The three of them together—" he stared into Rollison's face, his mouth working, his hands clenching and unclenching. "Rollison, I would kill them now if I knew where to find them. Hanging would be better than living like a pauper in a nightmare world peopled by fantasies—fantasies I've lived on while I've been away. But—I don't know where they are. They're too clever for me. My mind's gone; I feel bitter now, but in an hour's time I won't care. Nothing will matter, I just won't care."

"And they left you nothing?" asked Rollison.

"They left me the key of a furnished apartment in

58

Shaftesbury Avenue," said Charmion. "Furnished! It has a bed and a table and a chair. They left my wardrobe—at least I can sell my clothes!—and that was all. The rent of the apartment is paid for a month. One month."

Rollison shifted his position and took out his cigarette case. Charmion accepted another cigarette. There was silence for a short while, and then Rollison said:

"Why did you come to see me?"

"I don't quite know," said Charmion, slowly. "And yet —I do. Rollison, when I knew you before, you had grandiose ideas of right and wrong. I didn't agree with you. I don't know whether you're right or not, but I do know that you impressed me as believing in a square deal—for everyone."

"Yes?" said Rollison.

"Including—perhaps—me," said Charmion, hoarsely. "Rollison, much of the money, much of the property that I left behind, was mine, genuinely mine. Never mind the money those witless fools subscribed to the League. Set that aside—I was wealthy enough before that. These people—my wife, my brother, his wife— they've robbed me of more than money—they've robbed me of hope, Rollison. I want—" he broke off, and turned his head away. "Oh, what's the use?"

"Why don't you really say what you mean," said Rollison, quietly.

Charmion said, while looking out of the window:

"I'm wasting my time, I know that. There's no sense in staying. I don't know what got into my mind, but it was an obsession. Those whom I depended upon have betrayed me, Rollison. You—I thought that you might help me to find what was mine, to hound them down, to make them pay for what they've done. It's illegal, isn't it? It's crime—you fancied yourself as an enemy of crime. But, of course, it's absurd. Quite absurd. Yet—" he stood up suddenly and gripped Rollison's arm. "Rollison! I'm absolutely penniless, I must have help! Will you—"

Then he broke off again, as if the expression in Rollison's eyes had seared his lips.

CHAPTER VIII

ROLLISON ANSWERS

Charmion did not look into Rollison's eyes again, but turned towards the door, clutching his hat. As he reached the door he squared his shoulders, as if making some effort to regain his composure.

"Charmion," said Rollison, quietly.

The man put a hand on the door and began to open it.

"Charmion," said Rollison, "if you're in urgent need of money, I'll help you."

Charmion turned on his heel, and stared as if he could not understand.

"What?" he said. "What did you say?"

"If you're in urgent need of money," repeated Rollison, I'll see you through for a few weeks. Shall we say a hundred pounds?" He eyed the man levelly, waiting for the reaction, alert for every movement and expression.

"Are you—*ser*ious?"

"Yes," said Rollison. He put his hand to his pocket and took out his wallet; he extracted four five-pound notes and held them towards Charmion. "This is on account. You can have a cheque for the balance."

"It—it's unbelievable," said Charmion, his voice faltering. "I didn't seriously—" he stared towards the notes. "Rollison, why do you make such an offer? What are the conditions?"

"There are no conditions," said Rollison. "I'd like some information. You can give it or not. I won't make any stipulations."

"What information do you want?"

"The names and addresses of the three people you've mentioned," said Rollison, and went on deliberately: "Your wife's. Your brother's. His wife's."

"Why?"

"I want to find out where they are and what they're doing."

"You mean you'll do to them what you did to me?" asked Charmion, hoarsely. "You'll hound them down?"

"I want to find out where they are and what they're doing," said Rollison, "no more than that at first. And I'd like full particulars of what money and what securities you left behind you, and what power you gave them." He put the notes on the bookcase near the door, and added offhandedly: "Please yourself. It may be just a waste of time."

Charmion said, harshly:

"You can have their names, and if you find them—" He stopped, shrugging his shoulders and seemed to sag. "I don't quite understand you, Rollison. I remembered how you'd talked and what a high-minded hypocrite you liked to make yourself sound. I didn't think you were serious."

"There's no need to go into that," said Rollison. "If you've been tricked and cheated, and you're up against it, I'll help you financially. For the rest, that's my affair."

Charmion stared at him for fully ten seconds, then stepped towards the table and said:

"Lend me a pen, will you?"

Rollison took a fountain-pen from his pocket and a pad of notepaper from a bureau, and put them on the dining-table. Charmion wrote swiftly, apparently oblivious of his surroundings. Rollison went into the study, took his cheque-book from a drawer and wrote out a cheque, using a desk-pen. It was for eighty pounds, made out to 'Bearer'. When he returned to the other room, Charmion had finished writing.

"That's what you want," he said, looking up.

"Add your present address, will you?" asked Rollison.

"I have."

"What name have you gone under?"

"My own."

"Charmion?"

61

"Gilbert Abbott Charmion," said Charmion. "It was my real name, Rollison, I didn't borrow it. At Dartmoor they warned me of the consequences of registering anywhere under a false name. Rollison, what *is* in your mind? What are you going to do?"

"I don't quite know," said Rollison.

Charmion said with sudden vehemence: "I suppose as soon as my back's turned you'll telephone the police and tell them that I've been begging!"

"Don't talk nonsense!" snapped Rollison, surprised to find himself angry. "I won't follow you, I won't have you followed. I'll take you on trust—up to a point. That's all."

"I still don't believe it," said Charmion, slowly.

He stood up, put his hand forward a few inches, then withdrew it hurriedly. He looked very pale, but there was more life in his eyes than when he had come. "I won't try to say 'thanks'," he said. "My God, Rollison, it's fantastic! The irony of it! The only man to help me is the man who damned me."

He stopped again, and this time walked hurriedly to the door, his step brisk and his shoulders squared. He did not wait for Rollison to open the door, but let himself out.

Rollison watched him going down the stairs; he did not once look back.

Rollison closed the door softly, then stepped into the study. There was no sign of the bowler-hatted man in the street, nor of Sergeant Wilson. After a short while, Charmion appeared and walked towards the Piccadilly end of the Terrace.

Rollison watched him out of sight.

Then he turned and regarded the sawdust-filled effigy bag which had been the parody of the man named Guy. Next, he went into the dining-room and picked up the slip of paper on which Charmion had written the names and addresses. Charmion's writing, with many flourishes and yet precise, was difficult to read, but he distinguished the names.

Charles Edward Charmion, 18a, Ryall Street, Chelsea.
Winifred May Charmion,   do
Laura Charlotte Charmion, 41, Wilberforce Mansions,
                                Putney Hill, S.W.
My own address: Flatlet 5, 217a, Shaftesbury Avenue.

There followed a list of securities, all of them in reliable companies, of cash balances on current and deposit accounts at various joint-stock banks, and the brief statement that he had given his wife and brother full power of attorney. The total value of the securities and balances was a little over two hundred thousand pounds.

"A very pretty list," said Rollison to himself, "and a very pretty story, plausible and convincing. Either Charmion is an actor out of the ordinary or he's had a very raw deal. Which deal," he added, looking at the hole in the top of the bag, where the neck of the effigy had been fixed, "is just a preliminary effort. If he's told the truth, then someone is setting a really ugly trap for Charmion."

He wished that Jolly were back, for he felt the need for exchanging ideas with someone else. Charmion's visit had an unreal quality which troubled him. Too much of the affair was unreal, he could not get his feet on solid earth.

"The odd thing is," he mused, "that I feel sorry for Charmion. *Sorry* for Charmion! Jolly would say that they're making a guy out of me!"

Except that he had Charmion's address and had seen the man in the flesh and knew his story, he could make no further progress, and there was not much he could do. He felt the need of action. Everything was wrong; too many things happened off stage and left him frustrated, checkmated and—much though he disliked admitting it—bewildered.

"No straight runs," he said aloud, and then chided

himself for talking aloud. "I'll find out what I can about the other Charmions," he added. "I wonder who can give me the—" he paused, his eyes widened. "Mike Anderson, of course! He was on the Charmion case."

He lifted the telephone and rang the *Echo* office, only to learn that Anderson was out. He tried the reporter's flat, but there was no answer. He put on his hat, determined to call on him. But the telephone rang before he was out of the flat.

"Rollison speaking," he said, and immediately there was a torrent of words in broken English.

"*M'sieu*! I 'ave found you, eet ees a great relief! M'sieu, this ees Fifi; you know who I mean, *hein?* M'sieu Roll'son, you must please come, to 'Ilda's 'ome, yes, you recall 'Ilda? M'sieu, I do not know if I am on my seat or my front, I am so worreed, please come!"

"What's happened, Fifi?" asked Rollison.

"Oh, I cannot tell you over the telephone, m'sieu, eet ees too quick for that, please come at once. Shoe, 'e weel be waiting at the café for you. M'sieu, 'urry. I tell 'Ilda you weel soon be there, *hein?* Good, m'sieu, good!"

"Fifi—" began Rollison, urgently.

All he heard was the noise of the receiver being replaced, and it conveyed a sense of urgency, like Fifi's manner. He went into the study, took a small automatic from a water-proof bag in a drawer, relocked the drawer and slipped the gun into his pocket, then hurried down the stairs.

There was no taxi in the Terrace, but he found one in the rank opposite the Green Park. He gave the address and sat back in the cab. Something else had happened to Hilda, and it had come too quickly on the heels of Charmion's visit for him to assess the possibilities. Fifi's excited summons had been anything but assuring. It was like everything in the affair; it whetted his appetite and then left him unsatisfied. It was conceivable that when he reached Mile End it would prove a false alarm, and he would find Fifi all smiles and apologies, her husband glum and reproachful.

At Piccadilly Circus he saw Jolly.

His man was walking with the package under his arm, his expression portentous; Rollison imagined that he had some news. But the taxi was in a stream of traffic and he could not stop to pick Jolly up. Even if he told the driver to turn back he would lose valuable time.

The journey took twenty-five minutes.

Before it was over Rollison was in a sweat of apprehension, reading far more into Fifi's summons than she had put into words; the traffic was thick, and it was impossible to make good speed, while the driver insisted on keeping to the direct route instead of trying short cuts. Hardly knowing what to expect, Rollison was on the pavement outside the restaurant before the taxi had stopped. He heard the man call: " 'Ere, wot abaht—"

"Wait!" called Rollison, and pushed open the door.

Every bench was empty, and there was no sound except the fall of his own footsteps on the polished linoleum.

"Fifi!" he called, but received no answer. "Joe!" He called their names alternately as he looked into the empty kitchen, freshly-cleaned—there was a pail of water in one corner with a scrubbing brush and a floorcloth; evidently someone had been interrupted in the middle of cleaning and had not been able to get back to finish the job.

The little parlour was also empty.

"I don't like it," said Rollison, aloud. The words seemed to come back at him mockingly and derisively. He lit a cigarette and walked along a narrow passage to a small outhouse, which led to a tiny yard. That, too, was empty.

The staircase led from the kitchen, for the building was very small, most of the space being taken up by the restaurant proper. There was little light; Rollison imagined that there was permanent black-out at the landing and in the rooms above. The stairs creaked as he climbed them, and he put his hands in his pocket round the butt of his gun.

Except for his footsteps there was no sound; the silence

was uncanny, as if the ghost of Fifi's laughter and high spirits, of her husband's deep voice and frequent guffaws, were near the Toff. He reached the landing and stood still, then called again:

"Fifi! Joe!"

No one answered.

"They've gone to see Hilda," muttered Rollison aloud. "I wonder if any of the neighbours know her address?"

He was not really satisfied with the explanation; he wanted it to be the right one, but was unconvinced even after he had looked through the small bedrooms and the bathroom, finding no one there, and no signs that anyone had been in the rooms recently. He turned to the landing and went slowly down the stairs; his eyes narrowed in the gloom.

He tripped over something.

He lost his footing, grabbed at the handrail, missed that, and went sprawling downwards, his hands scraping against the wall. He realized that there had been a string stretched across the stairs, *and that it had been fixed while he had been on the upper floor.*

He concentrated on breaking his fall as best he could; he slid down a step at a time, bruising his buttocks and thighs, but when he reached the bottom he was not seriously hurt. He was able to put his right hand to his pocket quickly, but before he could grip the gun someone struck him.

It had the same farcical element as the rest of the business; it was with a pillow, billowy and soft, making him breathless, but not hurting him. He was buffeted, by someone he could not see, about the head and shoulders. He sneezed when feather dust got into his nostrils. Had he been on his feet he might have fought against it, but could only try to protect his face against the furious buffeting. It went on until he began to gasp for breath and his lungs seemed ready to burst. He could not utter a word as he tried, without success, to get out of the way of the pillow.

He began to gulp; there was too much dust and he

66

didn't get time to breathe; he felt that he must have air or else collapse. Yet it did not cease. He tried to get to his feet, but when he reached one knee someone pushed him in the back and he sprawled forward again. He felt as if he were suffocating, and into his mind there sprang the possibility that they were deliberately trying to kill him this way. He gasped and choked, but every time he fought his way clear another buffet caught him in the face and he gulped down dust which blocked his nostrils and constricted his throat.

He knew that he could not retain consciousness much longer; and then he stopped struggling, taking in a single gulp which made his breathing worse, but hoping that his assailant would think that he had fainted.

The buffeting continued.

The attempt to fox his opponent had not only failed, but made his plight more hopeless. Then, making a final effort to get to his feet, while that fighting, shadowy thing in front of him wrapped itself about his face like a warm, stifling blanket, he felt a greater pressure.

The pillow was over his face, being pressed against him, harder every moment. He could not breathe; his body heaved and twisted, but he could not breathe. Noises beat loudly and desperately in his ears, he felt his blood pounding, he imagined his tongue pressing itself against his teeth, forcing itself out.

Then he lost consciousness.

He recovered, not knowing where he was nor, for a while, what had happened. He was aware of a great thirst and a peculiar sense of warmth at his nose and the back of his throat. Then as the first realization of what had happened came back, he sat abruptly and looked about him.

He was on the floor of a small room—a bedroom, with an iron bedstead against one wall. There was only just room for him on the floor between the bed and the fire-place, which was filled with red crêpe paper. The room smelt frowsy, but that, he knew, might be because of the dust still in his nostrils.

There was a sound not far away which he did not immediately identify; then he realized that it was someone knocking. He wished it would stop. He buried his face in his hands, for his head was aching and there was a sense of strain at the back of his neck. He could not see his face, and when he looked down and saw his body he did not think, at first, that there was anything unusual; then he realized with a sense of shock that he had on only his pants and singlet.

"Clothes." He gulped the word, and looked about him. They were draped over the end of the bed; he could see the end of the trousers and one of the coat sleeves. "Oh." He was relieved although puzzled. The knocking continued and he said irritably: "Be quiet!"

There was a small window—high in one wall, admitting a shaft of sunlight which shone upon the dust that was everywhere; a coating of it was over his legs and arms, the floor gave off a small cloud when he moved to take a grip on the side of the bed, to pull himself to his feet. The banging became louder, and there was another sound—hurrying footsteps, which he thought were those of two or three men. They seemed a long way off.

If there were only a drink of water, he thought, he would feel ten times better. The aching in his head, the constriction at his throat, the dryness of his lips and mouth—all of them would be eased if he could only get some water. He realized that his eyes were half-closed and that he had difficulty in keeping them open at all. The senselessness of the attack, the lack of finality, occurred to him afresh and made him frown, but his main concern was still the need of something to drink.

He managed to pull himself to his feet, then looked down at the bed.

He stood motionless.

He forgot his need of water, the hurrying footsteps and the banging, the fantastic assault at the foot of the stairs at Fifi's and Joe's. The shaft of sunlight coming through the window shone upon gold hair, spread out on a bolster—a pillow, with feathers strewn all over it, was on the side of the bed.

It was beautiful hair, especially in the sun; it made a panoply of beauty for a hideous thing—a woman's face, mauve and blue and purple in patches, with the tongue poking out and the mouth distended, the eyes wide open and protruding.

An age seemed to pass as he stared down.

The woman wore a night-dress, rucked about her; the bedclothes were heaped against the wall, as though two people had been struggling. Her neck was swollen horribly, and thus threw into macabre contrast the creamy pallor of her shoulders, where the nightdress had been ripped away, and the whiteness of her limbs. In one hand she clutched a corner of the half-empty pillow. The feathers were all about her, a snowy blanket mercifully hiding the worst of her expression.

He did not recognize her, although he felt sure that she was Hilda Brent.

He did not recognize the voices which he heard outside the door, although he had little doubt that they belonged to policemen, and confirmation was not long coming, for a man said harshly:

"Open this door! Open this door, in the name of the law!"

Rollison looked, not at the door, but at the tiny window.

CHAPTER IX

NO ESCAPE
BY THE WINDOW

The window was too small; there was no chance of escaping by it, and even if he tried the door, a flimsy one already shaking under the weight of new blows, was not likely to hold long enough.

There was no time, either, to put on his clothes.

He stared again at the murdered woman, and knew exactly what had been planned for him. Not one man in a thousand would believe the truth. He was caught, redhanded, in a crime he had not committed, a crime which would arouse a deep horror in all who heard of it.

The fact did not have a demoralizing effect; instead, it made him feel steadier, and he found his voice.

"All right, don't break the door down!"

His voice was hoarse, but made the men on the other side of the door stop; one of them called out:

"What's that?"

"Wait a minute!" called Rollison. He looked round and saw a glass of water—its surface covered with dust—on the mantelpiece. He scooped some of the dust off with his finger, and rinsed his mouth out. He tried to think, desperately anxious to gain time.

Then he had another shock: the door was bolted on the inside, as well as locked. He stepped forward, while impatient voices sounded again, and drew the bolt back; he hoped to do it without making a noise, but it squeaked, and then stuck, only to move finally with a sharp noise which must have told the men outside what he was doing.

"Hurry up!" a man called, angrily.

Rollison turned the key; as he did so the door was thrust open and a uniformed policeman pushed him aside and strode past him. A second man, older and stolid, blocked the doorway.

The moment seemed to last for an age; it had a nightmare quality, a horror which was made worse by that shaft of sunlight shining on the woman's golden hair. Rollison stared at the policeman who had passed him, saw the man stand for a moment by the bed, then turn and face him. He saw an expression of savage rage on a square, homely countenance, an expression he might have shown had he made this discovery himself.

"Wha—" began the second man, and then stopped, for he was able to see past the Toff. His face also reflected horror, and then took on the same bleak fury.

Rollison spoke as clearly and crisply as he could.

"My name is Rollison—the Hon. Richard Rollison. I have no knowledge of who killed this woman. I want to get in touch with Superintendent Grice immediately."

"*You* want!" the first man snapped. "I should think—"

"*Rollison?*" said the man by the door, startled. "The Hon. Richard *Rollison?* You mean—the Toff?" His blue eyes were wide open and he peered at Rollison intently. Then, for the first time, Rollison caught sight of his face in a small mirror on the wall. He was covered with dust and feathers; no one would have recognized him.

"Yes," he said crisply. "I said Superintendent Grice, of Scotland Yard."

The man by the bed was the one in charge, and for the first time there was a relaxation in his tension and he blinked.

"Recognize him, Sam?"

"It *could* be the Toff," said Sam, bewilderedly.

"I don't care who he is," growled the first speaker. "He won't get away with this, not even if he knows the Chief Constable himself. If I had my way—"

Rollison said: "Someone killed that woman. I didn't. The longer you stand talking and wasting time, the more chance you'll give the murderer to get away. Never mind what you believe or what *I'll* get away with. Tell Superintendent Grice what has happened." He spoke sharply, hoping that his manner would carry sufficient authority; he saw the first faint doubt in the other's eyes.

"Better call the Yard, Sam. I'll look after this so-and-so."

"Ahoy, there! Anyone about?" A fresh voice called from below, one which Rollison thought familiar but which he did not immediately recognize. Footsteps sounded on the stairs. He wished he knew where he was, why there seemed so few people about, and why the police had hurried here and forced their way into the house.

"Who's that?" asked the first man. "Keep him out, Sam."

"Anyone *abooout*?" called the man below, and Rollison suddenly realized who it was.

In a few seconds, unless the policeman prevented him, Mike Anderson of the *Echo* would be in the passage; and probably he would have a camera with him. Rollison saw another facet of the diabolical cunning with which this had been planned.

"Keep him out!" hissed the first policeman.

Sam hurried downstairs, and an argument followed, the voice of Anderson sounding above the policeman's. Rollison stepped to the end of the bed and picked up his clothes.

"Leave that alone!" the policeman said.

Rollison ignored him, and drew on his trousers. The man glared but made no effort to stop him. Rollison slipped on his coat, and took out his cigarette case. In the other pocket he felt the automatic; it seemed that nothing had been taken. He lit the cigarette, then wished that he had not, for he wanted a drink more than ever. He knew that Sam would send for the Divisional men as well as Grice, and that the waiting period would soon be over but would Grice give him full support? On the face of it, there was a cut-and-dried case against him. He would have the greatest difficulty in proving what had happened, although two things might help. One was the

72

taxi-driver whom he had left outside the café; no one who planned such a crime as this would have left the man waiting. The other was the buffeting at the café; there must be traces of feathers to bear out his story.

The voices faded, the footsteps with them.

"Who sent for you?" Rollison demanded.

"You be quiet," the policeman said.

"Try to get it into your head that I have been framed. Work on that basis; get some kind of a report ready for your superior when he arrives."

"I heard you unbolt the door—and there's no way anyone could have got out of this room except *by* that door," the policeman said harshly.

Rollison gave up. It was useless to tell this man that by careful manipulation with the right tools, the bolt could have been moved from outside. As, of course, it had been.

The air of fantasy had gone; stark realism was upon him now the tenor of the case had altered. He remembered how, when he had first been hit by the pillow, that he thought it another fool's trick; also, when he had regained consciousness, he had thought that it had been another interim attack.

"Where is this?" he asked, after a long pause.

"I told you to be quiet!"

Rollison shrugged and stubbed out his cigarette, and then, while the other was looking at the pillow in the dead woman's hand, he heard a creaking movement near the door.

He snapped: "Constable, there's—"

The policeman turned swiftly, at the same time as a man appeared on the threshhold. Rollison moved swiftly towards him, then stopped short. The policeman grabbed his arm, while Mike Anderson stood gaping at the Toff.

"G-great Scott!" gasped Anderson. "Rolly, it is—"

He looked past Rollison, towards the bed, and his expression altered. He muttered something under his breath and then said to the constable:

"Who is she? Any idea?"

"Never you mind," said the policeman. "Who are you—that's more to the point."

"I'm from the *Echo*," Anderson said, and took out a card. He looked at Rollison and then away. Rollison could almost see his mind working.

"Well, you can't stay here," said the constable. "I wish—

More footsteps on the stairs heralded the arrival of Sam and, apparently; a third policeman. Rollison freed himself from the policeman's grip and went up to Anderson.

"Mike, this fellow's unfriendly, but you needn't be. I want some information about people named Charmion, once at Ryall Street, Chelsea, and Wilberforce Mansions, Putney. I'm not going to have much freedom of movement for the next couple of hours. See what you can do, will you?"

Anderson stared at him.

"Do I have to tell you that I didn't do this?" demanded Rollison. "For Pete's sake, don't act like a goat! Another thing—see Jolly and ask him to show you a wax face—wax face, got that? It's a good likeness of a man who calls himself Guy. If you can get a line on Guy—"

The arrival of Sam and another uniformed policeman made much further talk impossible.

"On the level?" Anderson demanded.

"Before you write this thing up, see Grice," urged Rollison. "By then I should be able to tell you more about it. Another thing—"

"That's enough," said his captor.

"All right," said Anderson. "I'll play."

Sam would have stopped him, but he eluded the man's grasp and hurried down the stairs.

Grice stood by the corner of the Assistant Commissioner's desk, the A.C. sat back in an easy chair looking preternaturally solemn, while Rollison sat opposite him, washed but still dishevelled and with feathers and dust over his hair and clothes.

Outside, dusk was falling and a wind was rising, whipping rain against the glass and sending the curtains billowing inwards. A draught played about Rollison's head, but he was hardly aware of it.

The A.C. was an oldish man whom he did not know well; his predecessor, who would have been as well-disposed as Grice, had taken a Regional Commissioner's post in the North. This man, Rollison knew, might be stubborn and unfriendly, or might just stick to the letter of the law. He was not likely to be greatly influenced by what Grice said, and might err on the side of severity because, amongst his friends and social acquaintances, there were many relations of Rollison's; leniency might bring accusations of old school tie comradeship.

"Your story is *quite* incredible, Mr. Rollison." He spoke softly, as if he loved using words and intended to get the fullest meaning out of each one; his voice rose and fell, mellow and attractive and yet, just then, more than exasperating. "In fact, I cannot remember hearing one which occasioned me more—er—scepticism."

"My story's true," said Rollison.

"I can hardly commit myself to an opinion on its truth; I can on its incredibility. I have received the reports of the police officers who were the first to release you from your strange predicament, and—" he tapped the tips of his fingers together softly—"I don't see that we can do other than detain you."

"Have you found the taxi-driver?" Rollison demanded. "Have you examined the staircase at the café? Or the bolt on the door?"

"The taxi-driver hasn't been found yet," Grice interpolated. "I looked at the bolt and staircase myself, Sir Hugh. The bolt has been scratched, although that is not conclusive. There are traces of feathers and feather-dust on the café staircase, although it's by no means smothered."

"Would there be feather-dust there normally?" asked Rollison. "And what about Joe Link and his wife?"

"They aren't there," said Grice.

75

Rollison stared: "Are you sure?"

"Yes. There's a notice on the door of the café saying that they will be away until further notice," Grice told him. It was impossible to guess what the Superintendent was thinking, for his face was expressionless and his eyes quite blank. "You feel sure that Fifi Link telephoned you?"

"I thought it was Fifi. It isn't difficult to fake a foreign accent, but it is to tell the real thing from an assumed one on the telephone. How long have they been gone?"

"Since morning."

"But the door was open when I got there!"

"You see," murmured the Assistant Commissioner, "only the Links could corroborate your story about the woman Brent—the story which you told the Superintendent earlier to-day, I mean. I really don't see—"

Rollison spoke, acidly.

"All right. Detain me, charge me, let the news get bandied about. If you charge me, you'll have to put me in dock; if you put me in dock I shall have the right to make a statement and to have a legal representative. It will be quite a sensation. The higher the jump, the greater the fall. But get on with it! I've been here so long that it won't make much difference, all London will have heard of it by now. Make it formal, make it official—and then for ever after wonder why you made such a thundering fool of yourself!"

"I see no point in being abusive," said the A.C., stiffly.

"Of course you don't!" Rollison pushed his chair back and stood up, stepping across the room and turning to face the others from the window. "The point is that by chance I know more about this business than Grice or any of his men, and I might get quick results. But don't worry about results, just keep to the regulations. Regulations! There was a time when I thought the safest thing I could do was to keep everything from the police until a case was cut-and-dried. I'm like Charmion, my mind's atrophied." He stepped back to the desk and, leaning one

76

hand on it and pointing the other at the A.C., who was so startled that he drew away, his lips parting, went on, "Do what you like with me, but find Fifi, find Joe Link, save them from the same fate as Hilda Brent. And there are others, perhaps dozens of others. Grice is on the fringe of it, but no more. Get past that fringe."

The telephone rang abruptly.

Rollison stopped and drew back. Grice looked at him meaningly, giving an almost imperceptible shake of his head. The A.C. shot Rollison an apprehensive glance and lifted the receiver.

"Yes, that's right," he said. "Yes . . . Downstairs. I see; that's good." He replaced the receiver and looked at Grice. "The taxi-driver is in the waiting-room, Superintendent. Er—what were you going to say, Rollison?"

Grice hesitated, then stepped towards the door. The A.C. nodded, dismissing him. The door closed behind him and Rollison ran his hand down the back of his head, then dropped into a chair and said, with a faint smile:

"I was letting off hot air, I'm afraid. You're wrong, you know. You shouldn't detain me. I'm the Aunt Sally, and the coconuts will come my way."

"Some have certainly struck," said the A.C. more mildly than might have been expected. "I am in a very difficult position. Of course, your reputation stands you in good stead, but—" He pressed a bell-push, and the door opened to admit a sergeant. "Take Mr. Rollison to Superintendent Grice's office, please, and stay with him there. I won't keep you any longer than I must," he added.

Rollison stood up. He fancied that there was a faint smile on the A.C.'s lips as the door closed, but the next half-hour dragged; the many urgent things pressing on his mind enraged him, and he could imagine no time when he could less afford to be idle.

When Rollison had left the larger room, the Assistant Commissioner waited for some time, frowning and, occasionally, reading a paragraph from Grice's report. He appeared to be in the throes of a considerable dilemma. When Grice returned, he spoke abruptly.

"Well? What does the taxi-driver say?"

"He bears out the story, sir."

"I see. You're well-disposed towards Rollison, aren't you, Grice?"

"I've known him for some years," said Grice cautiously, "and even without the taxi-driver's evidence I would be reluctant to think him capable of murder. On the other hand"—he paused, but as the A.C. did not speak, went on—"it is just possible that the taxi-driver has been bribed to make his statement. If it were anyone but Rollison—" he paused again, this time waiting until his chief spoke.

"If it were anyone but Rollison," said the A.C., "you would not consider taking his word. In spite of his past record, we can hardly give him his freedom unconditionally. We have to admit the possibility that he is being framed, but at the same time the *prima facie* evidence suggests that he might have visited this woman and then had a brainstorm. However, he *is* Rollison and we might be justified in taking a chance with him when with anyone else it would be impossible." He paused. "But we shall have to take extreme precautions. You think that with Rollison at liberty there is a greater chance of getting to the bottom of this business, because in your opinion one of the essential conditions of the criminals' plot is to have him under charge, isn't that so?" The A.C. tapped Grice's report.

"It is, sir," admitted Grice.

"That would justify us giving him rope in the event of a Home Office inquiry later," said the A.C., "but only if we have a secure hold on the other end of the rope. Have we a good man who can watch him?"

Grice said slowly: "It would need two, and if he discovered that he was being watched, and wanted to act on his own, he would probably shake them off."

"On the other hand, if he did elude the men, immediately he was found again we would have to bring him in." The A.C. grew decisive. "Detail the best men for the job, Grice, then tell Rollison that we are releasing him because of the taxi-driver's evidence. Say nothing more; we can judge by his actions whether there is any justification for the experiment, but we musn't stretch the point any farther."

"I see that, sir," said Grice, and added with obvious sincerity: "I think it's the right thing to do, and I appreciate it."

"I hope you're right," said the A.C., and nodded dismissal.

The blinds were down at the windows by which Rollison stood, and the room was stuffy. The sergeant waited impassively by the door. Every time footsteps sounded on the cement floor of the passage outside Rollison grew tense with expectancy, but each time they passed. He knew that if he were detained, whether under charge or not, he would find it hard to keep his temper.

But could he blame them if they held him?

He was obsessed by the fact that precious hours were passing when he needed to give all his attention to the problem of Charmion—or those who were also framing Charmion. He could not think clearly about it, even Charmion's visit was blurred in outline. He saw two Charmions, the man at the window of the Kettledrum and the man who had talked with such unrestrained passion in the flat. He thought of Guy, of Jolly's inquiries, of his suspicion that the man at the Kettledrum window had been made up to look like Charmion; and then he said aloud in a startled, almost angry voice:

"Not Charmion—Charmion's *brother!*"

Then the door opened and Grice came in.

CHAPTER X

BROTHER TO CHARMION

"You're all right," said Grice.

Rollison stared at and through him, seeing in his mind's eye the face at the window and obsessed with the idea that had come to him.

"Good," he said, absently. "Grice, I—*what's* that?"

"I thought you'd wake up to it soon," Grice said drily. "The taxi-driver remembers you. He waited outside for twenty minutes, and when you didn't turn up he had a look in the restaurant. All he remembered was feathers at the foot of the stairs. Then a man came out and paid his fare, so he went off."

"Well, well," said Rollison, backing to Grice's desk and leaning against it. "The flaw in the scheme was as obvious as that. He didn't recognize the man who paid him, did he?"

The description he gives isn't much help," Grice said. "It was pretty dark there, and a man of medium height, dark, with a round face, doesn't help us a great deal."

"No." Rollison took out his cigarette case and lit up. "So I'm taken on trust? I misjudged the A.C.," he added, "I thought he'd be the do-or-die type."

"The taxi-driver saved your bacon," said Grice, "although I helped just a little."

"Of course!" Rollison exclaimed. "I'm an oaf. One day I'll say 'thanks'. It shook me," he admitted. "I haven't felt like I did when I saw Hilda for a long time. It was Hilda Brent?"

"Yes."

"What else do you know?" Rollison asked.

"I can tell you where you were found and why the police arrived when they did," said Grice, "but are you as interested as all that? What were you saying when I came in just now?" When Rollison did not answer, he added: "You won't hold out on me now, surely?"

"I will not!" Rollison assured him. "It's the old, old story—is it a workable theory or is it just a flight of fancy?" He proved that he was more interested in what he had thought of Charmion's brother than in what Grice could tell him by plunging into the story, etching in the details and the reasons for the possibility that Charmion's brother, his wife, and Charmion's wife also, were in this plot and were working against both him and Charmion.

Grice frowned and sat down at his desk, which was scrupulously tidy. The wind blustered and shrieked outside, and not far off there was a noise, as if a sign were banging against its support. The sergeant waited by the door, studying a report which he had picked up when Grice had entered.

"Do you really think much of it?" demanded the Superintendent quietly. "Or is it just a bright idea?"

"I don't know," admitted Rollison. "Be wary of ideas, for they so often make you take the wrong turning. All the same, he was uncannily like Charmion was seven years ago. Where can we find out about him? He didn't appear in the case, as far as I can remember, but there might be something in police records about him. Will you look?"

Grice glanced at the sergeant: "Go along to Records," he said, "and bring all the files relative to the Charmion case, Forbes." When the man had gone he added to Rollison: "I've been checking on the earlier attack on Hilda Brent and those she said were made on her children. I can't find any evidence that any was criminal, except the attack on her in the street, and there isn't much help to be got from that. The thing is—"

Rollison said: "Motive, yes. Why kill her? Not simply to make a case against me. You'd have a job to convince any coroner or jury of that one."

"Do you believe that's the motive?" demanded Grice.

Rollison shook his head.

"I do not. But if it weren't, then they needed to kill Hilda for some other potent reason. They've spirited Fifi and Joe away for the same purpose—unless they managed to persuade them to go away somewhere, and I don't think it's likely. They were greatly concerned about Hilda and anxious that I should do something for her. Have you a call out for them?"

"Of course."

"What about Hilda's children?"

"One's in hospital, getting over the car accident," Grice told him. "The other two are being looked after by her husband's mother. The mother had the children yesterday morning, and neighbours arranged to look in on Hilda every hour or two, to see that she was all right. They had wanted her to stay in hospital, but she had insisted on coming out."

Rollison said, swiftly:

"Why? Did she say?"

"Does that matter?" asked Grice.

"Of course it matters! There was a motive for her murder; there was a motive for her wanting to come out of hospital. They might be related. Will you check up on what she said when she insited on returning to the house?"

Grice brushed a hand slowly across his forhead.

"What an amazing fellow you are for making the obscure seem obvious! Yes, I'll see if there was anything worth while; you can leave that side of it to me." Grice made a note on a writing pad, then went on: "Hilda Brent lived in a street behind the Mile End Road, not a hundred yards from the Links' restaurant. The buildings between the back of the restaurant and the back of the house where Hilda was living are all empty—they were condemned—and Hilda's is the only habitable one, on her side of the road, for a stretch of fifty yards or more. We can only assume that you were carried that way and no one saw you—or else they were bribed or persuaded to be silent."

Rollison nodded, only half of his mind on that item of news.

"And the police arrived because—"

"A neighbour reported hearing screams."

"There weren't many neighbours about when the police arrived, were there?"

"There were enough," said Grice. "We'd cleared them away by the time you were brought out. Well, that's as far as we can go for the time being, Rolly, except—what was it you asked Anderson to do?"

"Find out what he could about the Charmions."

"Wasn't there something said about a wax face?"

"Oh, that?" exclaimed Rollison. "Haven't I told you about it? I should have done," he added, and explained.

Then the sergeant brought in the files on the Charmion case, but there was no mention of the man's relatives.

It was after nine o'clock when Rollison reached his flat, having telephoned Jolly from the Yard. Jolly was agog when Rollison arrived, but he had nothing of great interest to report, except that his friend Saul Lauriston had examined the face and the artificial eyes, and hoped to have some news by the morning. For the rest—

"Mr. Anderson called, sir, and said that he would look in again about ten o'clock. Mr. Anderson of the *Echo*, I mean."

"What did he tell you?"

"Nothing at all, sir."

"Not a word?"

"He simply asked whether you were in, and when I told him that I expected you at any time, he gave me that message. Should he have told me anything, sir?"

"No," said Rollison. "But he might have done. He didn't say that I sent him?"

"No." Jolly looked puzzled, and a little later, after Rollison had told him what had happened—Rollison had changed while talking—he looked worried and more doleful than ever. It was Jolly's habit to look glum, but Rollison believed he was genuinely worried.

Rollison, eating a snack which his man had prepared for him, looked up with one eyebrow raised, and said gently:

"Not a nice case, Jolly, is it?"

Jolly said: "I have no wish to appear unduly pessimistic, sir, nor to invite the risk of being dubbed a Jonah, but I have rarely known so unpleasant an affair. There is an atmosphere of unreality about it, a touch of the macabre, a beastliness which—but then, I need hardly tell *you*, sir."

"No-o," mused Rollison. "And yet it has its bright side, I suppose. We haven't found it yet." He frowned. "We haven't found Fifi or Joe Link, either. I'd give a lot to know that they were safe. Deep waters, Jolly."

"That is of less consequence, sir, than the fact that the sea is uncharted," said Jolly sombrely.

"Our defences are dispersed, which is what the enemy's after," Rollison said. "I don't know that I like jobs where we don't know who we're fighting. There's certainly been a powerful effort to make us think we're fighting Charmion—or else to make us think we're not," he added, and shot his man a speculative glance. "What do you make of Charmion's visit?"

"He *could* have come to persuade you, falsely, that he is not in the affair, sir."

"Presenting a refinement of the double-cross?" Rollison looked at the clock on the mantelpiece; it was a quarter to ten. "I'll give Anderson half an hour, and if he hasn't arrived by then—"

"What will you do, sir?" asked Jolly, when Rollison paused.

"Go to see Charmion," said Rollison, "and make sure that he's in his furnished apartment."

At a quarter past ten there was no sign of the reporter and Rollison went out, leaving instructions with Jolly to ask Grice to send men to the Shaftesbury Avenue house if he did not return by midnight. He did not think it likely that there would be serious trouble at the furnished apartments which had so disgusted Charmion, but he had transferred his gun from one jacket to the other, and he felt it against his side as he walked as quickly as the black-out would allow to Piccadilly Circus.

Grice's men followed him, but did not betray themselves.

The squalls of rain had stopped but the wind was high, howling and whining, occasionally sending clouds of mist against Rollison's face. Traffic crawled, lights were reflected on the greasy roads and wet pavements. At the Circus, he went down the subway and came up at the end of Shaftesbury Avenue—and then, for no apparent reason—he remembered Sergeant Wilson, who had followed the bowler-hatted man but of whom Grice had said nothing.

"Odd," decided Rollison, *sotto voce*.

He inquired at a little café, which was open, for Number 217a, and was directed further along the Avenue. The building where Charmion was living was a large one, with wide-fronted shops on the ground floor, office suites on the first and second, and then furnished apartments approached by a narrow wooden staircase. The landings were illuminated by dim blue lights; Flat 5, he found, was on the top floor. As he mounted the last flight of stairs he was reminded vividly of his search of Fifi's rooms, and he kept his hand on his gun.

Standing on the landing, he saw that there was only one flat on that floor—the '5' was marked clearly in white on a dark door. He heard voices—a man's and a woman's. He did not know why he was surprised at hearing a woman's. He was about to ring the bell when he heard a door open and the voices grew louder. He stepped aside; there was a note in one of the voices which struck a familiar chord, and made him move swiftly back into the shadows of a corner.

The door opened.

"Yes, yes," the woman said, "I know; I'll do what I can." Rollison kept quite still; he saw her clearly as the light from Charmion's flat shone upon her. She was clad in a macintosh too large for her, and wore a wide-brimmed hat, but there was no mistaking her.

Charmion, his face set but his eyes glittering, watched her as she began to go down the stairs, while Rollison tried to digest this new development—the fact that *Georgina Scott* had visited Charmion. As he stared, unseen by Charmion, he remembered how surprisingly she had been affected by the man's name, written in fading ink, on the card at the Kettledrum.

CHAPTER XI

ACCIDENT OR DESIGN?

Rollison kept quite still.

He wanted Charmion to go in and close the door, for he was on tenterhooks to follow Georgina, whose footsteps were getting fainter and fainter.

So long did Charmion stand by the door, after all chance of seeing Georgina had gone, that the Toff wondered whether it were by accident or design. He had not been stealthy in his approach to the top floor, and the man might have heard him coming, and suspect that he was waiting in the shadows. Then Charmion turned and looked towards him; the room light was behind the man, whose face was in shadow; it looked like a death's head, except for the odd, unnatural brilliance of the eyes. That was a trick of the faint blue light in front of him, but it was none the less effective.

"Why don't you come out?" asked Charmion. His voice sounded tired. "Why must you play such foolish tricks?"

He could not possibly see the Toff, who did not move, believing then that Charmion was not sure of himself.

"Oh, come out!" snapped Charmion. The Toff started to emerge from his corner but suddenly stood rigid, hardly breathing, for another man moved from the opposite corner.

The man went forward with heavy tread; Rollison could not see his face, but he recognized the sturdy figure, while the voice would have betrayed Mike Anderson anywhere.

"Have you got eyes in the dark?" he asked.

"Who are you?" Charmion demanded. He seemed very tired.

"I'm from the Press," said Anderson, "just paying a little call, Charmion."

"What interest has the Press in me?"

"What interest have you in the Press?" retorted Anderson. It was a superficially bright remark, and Rollison believed he made it because he wanted to gain time. Neither of them could have anticipated the oath which shot from Charmion's lips, although Rollison was carried, mentally, away from the landing to his own flat, where he had looked down upon Charmion and the man had spoken with such passion.

"I *hate* the Press!" cried Charmion. "Every man working on it, every foul-minded reporter, every filthy sub-editor's pencil, every machine, every inch of paper! Do you understand? I hate the Press!"

"Don't you think we'd do better inside?" interrupted Anderson. "You have neighbours."

After a pause, Charmion said:

"What do you want from me?"

"A story," said Anderson.

"I have no desire for the cheap publicity that you can give me," said Charmion. "I want to forget what happened seven years ago, but you—of course, *you* will breathe into the corpse of the past and give it a life that will send shudders of delighted horror down the backs of your witless readers. I have no time for the Press."

"You've time for me," said Anderson, grimly.

"I have no—"

"Because I've just seen your wife," said Anderson.

Charmion raised one hand as far as his chest, the fist clenched. He backed into the room, so that he looked as he had at Rollison's flat, colourless and faded, a man who had lost all interest in life but who was suddenly filled with a dread which might goad into vigorous, artificial life.

"Are you—*lying?*" His voice was strangled.

"I've just seen your wife," repeated Anderson.

There was another pause, and during it the Toff faced

the Solomon's choice ahead of him. If he revealed himself and went in the apartment with Anderson he might learn much; but he wanted to find Georgina. All hope of following her had gone, but she might have gone straight home, and be easily persuaded to talk. Anderson, of course, knew that he was there; the blue light had been enough to reveal his features, and his approach could not have been concealed from the landing. Yet Anderson preferred to say nothing.

"You'd better come in," said Charmion, still wearily, and stood aside.

Anderson went through, and the door closed on them. Rollison waited only until he heard the second door close, then hurried down the stairs, running when he reached the second landing. He rushed out of the door of the building, drew up when he saw a shadowy figure passing, and heard a casual American voice ask him where in hell he was going. Then a taxi drew near.

"Taxi!" Rollison called, and the driver pulled in towards the curb, a few yards ahead of Rollison, who hurried towards it. "Twenty-nine, Portman Place," said Rollison, and the door slammed behind him.

Thus he eluded Grice's men, who 'phoned a report immediately. Grice told them to go to Gresham Terrace and report as soon as Rollison returned.

Rollison sat back, glad of a chance for reflection, yet not certain that he had made a wise choice. Jolly had hit the nail on the head when he had said that in this affair there was no time to concentrate upon any single issue; too many things happened simultaneously.

Had Anderson seen Charmion's wife? Or had he said so simply to force an interview? He had talked as if the fact that Charmion was married had been a well-known one; but, as far as Rollison knew, he could only have learned of it as a result of his investigations after his visit to Hilda's room.

"He's no fool," Rollison reflected. He lit a cigarette, then closed his eyes, to concentrate upon Georgina. It

89

was remarkable what little he knew about Georgina Scott; but then, there was no reason why he should know much.

Her mother was a quiet, languorous woman, beautiful in a very different way from Georgina, with none of her daughter's woolliness of mind and word. Sir Roland Blanding was, in fact, her stepfather, who had made his money in patent foods and was now at the Ministry of Agriculture. The family was wealthy—but it was only after reflection that Rollison realized he did not know who Georgina's real father was, only that her mother had married Blanding some five years before, and that it had caused much comment, for Blanding had been eligible in every way.

"Of course," mused Rollison, "there's no reason why Georgina's father should have been anything but worthy, but I don't like little mysteries." He opened his eyes when the cab slowed down, surprised to find himself in Portman Place. The driver was going slowly, trying to see the numbers painted on the pillars at the porches of the houses.

Rollison tapped on the glass partition.

"All right. I'll find it," he said.

"We just passed twenty-one," said the cabby, "it'll be about 'ere, sir." He leaned out of his seat and opened the door, and Rollison climbed out, paid him, and stood in the silence as the cab moved off.

Some distance away the hum of traffic made a faint background of sound, yet seemed to serve chiefly to emphasize the quietude. So did the faint strains of music, presumably from a radio, which filtered from behind the curtained windows. The wind and rain had stopped, although it was only a brief lull, and as Rollison found the porch of Number 29 a gust of wind came whining and tearing about the street, whipping his hat from his head. He saved it. The wind took his breath away and made him swing round, to turn his back to it. Then it went away up the street, moaning as if trying to find some precious thing that it had lost, leaving the street in a brooding silence.

"I wonder if she's back yet?" Rollison said aloud.

Georgina might have gone elsewhere, he knew, so this might be a completely wasted visit; probably he would serve his purpose best by knocking and inquiring from her. But he was reluctant to do that and waited for three more gusts of wind before, in the fourth lull, he heard footsteps approaching him.

Turning, he saw the beam of a small torch pointing towards the pavement and shining on neat shoes and well-turned legs, each more clearly defined in turn as the newcomer drew nearer; he thought it was probably Georgina, although he could see nothing above her knees. Another gust of wind made her stop, sending her skirts swirling about her thighs; but when it had gone she hurried on, shone the torch towards the four stone steps of the house, and mounted them. It was Georgina.

"Shall I show myself now?" Rollison asked himself.

Georgina inserted a key in the lock; the silence was deep enough for him to hear that clearly. If he called her, out of the darkness, he would give her a fright and she might be more prone to talk; on the other hand, a fright might make her obstinate and give her time to think about the reason for his questions. It would be better to pretend that he knew nothing of where she had been, but try to get her story in an indirect way. So he waited for the door to open; a faint light shone from the hall, putting her figure in clear silhouette.

That was not all.

" 'Gina!" exclaimed a man's youthful voice, and the door remained open. Georgina poised on the threshold, staring at someone whom Rollison could not see.

" 'Gina!" repeated the man, agitatedly. "I've been waiting for an hour!"

"Oh," said Georgina, in so low a voice that Rollison could hardly hear the words, "I'm sorry."

She went in; a man's shadow appeared on the porch, a

hand gripped the side of the door, and then it closed; sight and sound of them disappeared, and another gust of wind swept along the street in its melancholy quest.

"So," murmured Rollison somewhat inanely. "An anxious boy-friend."

He waited for two or three minutes, so that his arrival would not appear too great a coincidence, and then went up the steps and rang the bell. There was a long delay, and he rang three times before a maid answered the door; Rollison thought that she looked as if she had been awakened from a sleep, for her hair was ruffled and her small white cap on one side; her eyes were bleary. She was hardly civil.

"I want to see Miss Scott," said Rollison crisply.

"Oo?" demanded the maid, puzzling Rollison, for Blanding was not a man to allow shortcomings amongst his staff. "Oh, Miss Georgina. She ain't in."

"Isn't she?" asked Rollison, sharply. He stepped past her, into the narrow hall, and took a card from his pocket. "Tell her that I am waiting, will you, and be quick!"

"But—" the maid began, and then a door opened along the passage and Georgina appeared, while the young man's voice came from the room, protestingly.

"But confound it, 'Gina—"

"It's no good Bob," said 'Gina, dully, "I'm too tired to think about anything to-night."

"Miss Georgina—" began the maid.

"'Gina," said Rollison, stepping forward and smiling at Georgina, who turned and stared at him. There was no doubt at all that she was startled, that of all people in the world Rollison was the last she wanted to see. It was a vivid, revealing flash, and although it faded quickly and she forced a smile, she would never convince Rollison that she was pleased to see him. And—

She was *frightened*.

"Why, Rolly!" she said, and her teeth flashed in the mechanical smile. "What on earth are you doing here so late?"

92

"Is it ever too late to wish to see you?" asked Rollison, amiably.

"Don't be an ass!" Georgina was making a real attempt to appear normal, and Rollison admired her for it.

Framed in the doorwar of the room on the right was the young man, personable-looking, obviously dissatisfied, frowning a little and, quite clearly, wondering what the devil this handsome stranger was doing here so late at night. The maid stood by the front door, prepared to open it at a word from Georgina.

Georgina looked towards her, and said sharply:

"You may go, May." The maid pouted, but went off, and Georgina shrugged; there was exasperation in her manner, as if she were tired of dealing with recalcitrant servants. "What do you really want, Rolly? Oh, I—this is Bob Moor. Bob, you probably know Richard Rollison."

Moor stared into Rollison's face, his eyes taking on a hint of wonderment, almost incredulity—there was something naive in his wide-eyed appraisal.

"Rollison!" exclaimed Moor. "You mean—I mean—are you the—"

"Bob!" exclaimed Georgina. She broke in simply to prevent the word "Toff" from being uttered, and Rollison was acutely conscious of Georgina's underlying fear. She was breathing heavily, and fighting a losing battle against revealing her perturbation. "Bob, come round in the morning, will you? Rolly, I'm absolutely *exhausted*, I'm tired out; oh, it's been such a *wicked* day. I'm sure I shall dream all night!" She shuddered, realistically; only the expression in her eyes told Rollison that she was lying desperately. "Perhaps you'll give me a ring in the morning, too, Rolly?"

"But—" began Moor.

"I won't keep you five minutes," Rollison promised her, earnestly.

"Look here, you can't go like this!" broke in Moor, and any doubt that he was as much on edge as Georgina faded completely. " 'Gina, you must be reasonable! Mr. Rollison will probably—"

"Oh, don't pester me!" cried Georgina. "Why don't you go home? I'm tired of talking, I've a dreadful headache, I can hardly keep my eyes open! I won't say another word to-night, do you hear? Not another word!"

And then, tears flooding her eyes, she turned and blundered towards the stairs, beginning to run once she reached them, and not looking back.

Moor stood outlined against the doorway, wide-eyed, staring first at the girl and then, as she disappeared round a bend in the stairs, towards the Toff.

CHAPTER XII

MR. ROBERT MOOR
AND ANOTHER

"I—I just can't understand it!" exclaimed Moor. "It beats me—it absolutely beats me!"

His eyes, large and blue and innocent, were turned towards Rollison, who was taking out his cigarette case. Moor accepted a cigarette and they lit up.

"I—I'm all at sea," continued Moor. "I say—you *are* the Toff, aren't you?"

"Yes," said Rollison. He had little time for false modesty, and he knew that hero-worship might be outweighed, then, by the urgency of the situation. "What's the trouble, do you know?"

"I don't really. Georgina seems to have gone completely bats!" Moor was smoking his cigarette too quickly. "Did you want to see her urgently?"

"Yes," said Rollison, "and it's more urgent than ever, now." He looked about the hall and saw a bell-push. He pressed it, while Moor stared at him. "You must know about the trouble."

"We-ell—yes, I suppose I do." Moor was nervous. "That is, she's frightened about something, but she won't tell me what it is. I can't understand it. Why, she's altered completely in a few hours! I saw her this morning, and—"

"What time this morning?" asked Rollison.

Moor looked away from him, and then smiled, a faintly abashed smile. It made him look a very pleasant young man indeed and, oddly, it also made him seem older than he had been while so perturbed and serious. "It was soon after nine. I came round and strolled with her to Lewis Street, where she works these days. I—er—I'm on leave, you see, and I'm rather at a loose end."

'Except,' thought Rollison, for 'dancing attendance on Georgina.' There might be many worse things than that, and this young man looked wholesome, the type to appeal to her. He had fair, rather fine hair that curled, and his fresh complexion was slightly tanned. His blue eyes—astonishingly clear—were fringed with long, fair lashes. He was trying to grow a moustache, which would never really mature.

"She was right as rain then," said Moor. "But at lunch-time she dashed off after about three minutes—wouldn't even stay to eat, and I'd—"

"Did she say why she was in a hurry?" asked Rollison, but before Moor could answer a swing door opened on the right of the hall and the maid appeared. She had tidied her hair and straightened her cap, and she looked a little self-conscious. "Yes, sir?"

"I want you to take a message to Miss Georgina," said Rollison. "Tell her that it is most important that I should see her for five minutes."

This time the maid did not argue, but said, "Yes, sir," and turned away at once. Rollison waited until she was out of earshot, and then said quietly:

"Did she?"

"What?" asked Moor. "Oh, say she—why she was in a hurry? No, she didn't explain at all. She just told me that something rather unexpected had cropped up and that she couldn't stay. It was at the Waldorf. Before I could persuade her she'd gone off. I rang her up three times at her office, but either she wasn't there or she wouldn't speak to me. I *can't* believe she wouldn't come to the 'phone," added Moor, earnestly. "I mean, we—" he hesitated and then went on in a rush of confidence "—we're practically engaged!"

'Practically,' thought Rollison, would not cut a great deal of ice with Georgina, who had been thrice engaged already. Obviously Moor was her present favourite, and it was not like Georgina to cut a man as she had apparently cut him. It was not, simply, a question of 'off with the old and on with the new'; Georgina might change her affections, but she would always be very nice about it.

"I see," mused Rollison. "She was in a hurry at lunch and—upset?"

"Well, she did seem a bit put out, but nothing like she is now," said Moor. "When I did manage to get her on the 'phone, earlier this evening, she said she would see me at half-past nine. She was in a hurry, then, but I thought she sounded more composed than she had done earlier."

"But she was late," murmured Rollison. "That's all you know?"

"Absolutely everything," said Moor earnestly. "It's shaken me. Oh, there's one other thing! When she did get in to-night, she'd obviously forgotten that I was going to be here. She seemed thoroughly upset—she was frightened. I asked her why, and she said something about serious trouble and there was nothing I could do to help her. That—er—that's why I was so pleased to see you."

Rollison smiled, absently.

"Having heard of the Toff? Never get yourself a reputation, it always rebounds. Did she say anything to suggest that her bother might be the kind in which I could help?"

"Well, no; but—" Moor broke off. "Oh, I don't know! But there is something wrong, Mr. Rollison. I don't understand how anything could have affected 'Gina like this, but—look here, can you do anything? You must know something about it, or you wouldn't be here."

"I can only try," said Rollison.

The maid returned, still prim, but with her face set firmly; Rollison read Georgina's answer in the girl's expression, and hardly needed to hear the quiet:

"Miss Georgina regrets she cannot see you to-night, sir."

"Oh, damn!" exclaimed Moor. "I—good Lord!"

"Sir!" exclaimed the maid. "Sir!"

She stood staring at Rollison's back, and Moor stared, equally astonished; for Rollison was half-way up the stairs. He reached the landing, looked along the darkened passages, and saw a sliver of light at the foot of one door. The maid's footsteps pattered urgently up the stairs in his wake. He strode along to the room where there was a light, and tapped sharply.

"What is it *now?*" demanded Georgina; her voice was taut, almost hysterical.

"Put a wrap on," said Rollison, opening the door an inch. "I'm coming in, 'Gina."

"Miss Georgina!" gasped the maid.

Rollison pushed the door wider open and stepped inside.

Georgina was standing in front of a dressing-table in a satin slip, her wavy auburn hair over her shoulders; she looked quite lovely, except for the expression in her eyes; it was akin to terror, and Rollison hated the sight of it.

"You've got no right to do this!" the maid began, angrily. "If you don't go I—I'll call the police!"

Rollison turned and looked at her.

"It's all right," he said. "You can wait here, if you want to." He left the door open and, stepping towards the bed, sat on the edge. He picked up a dressing-gown from the foot-panel, and held it out to Georgina. She took it mechanically, her eyes on him all the time. "No, 'Gina," said Rollison, rallying her calmly, "you're not getting anywhere behaving like this, you know. What's the trouble?"

Georgina gasped: "What—what do you want?"

"All I wanted to find out was whether you'd seen the name 'Charmion' anywhere again?" said Rollison. "That's all, but now—why so worried, 'Gina? And why can't I help?"

The maid's expression had altered; she stood by the door but was no longer so grim as she had been; it was almost as if she were now on the Toff's side.

Georgina put the dressing-gown on, but did not speak.

"Well?" asked Rollison, gently.

"I—I can't tell you anything," mumbled Georgina. "It

—it's nothing to do with you, it's personal. Rolly, don't worry me, *please*."

"But I must—" began Rollison.

"And what must you do?" demanded a man from the passage.

It was a firm voice, that of a man who knew his mind; and its owner came in. He was tall and well-built, wearing an overcoat of excellent cut, and carrying a hat and gloves. His full, florid face was purposeful, and his blue eyes were very direct and hard. Rollison had seen him before and recognized Roland Blanding; the tag 'strong man' had often been applied to Blanding, and his appearance justified it. He walked with a firm, deliberate tread, but made little or no sound, only partly because of the thick carpet. The Toff might have been justified in thinking that Blanding had approached stealthily; but then, in such circumstances, Blanding would have been fully justified in doing so.

"Father!" exclaimed Georgina; it was, somehow, like her to utter just that word, and then to turn and collapse on the dressing-table, burying her head in her arms and beginning to sob.

"Well?" Blanding's lips hardly moved; they were well-shaped but thin, and tight set.

Rollison said: "You know me, perhaps?"

"I do not," said Blanding crisply. "Nor do I know what right you have to force yourself into my daughter's room. Get out!"

"Later," said Rollison, standing up. "I think—"

"I do not know who you are, and don't care," said Blanding. "I do know that unless you are out of this room in thirty seconds, I shall throw you out. And if you are not—"

Rollison said: "If I go out of here, may you and I have a talk?"

"We may not!" snapped Blanding. "I have told you to get out."

"Oh," said Rollison, a little foolishly. "A showdown?"

He sat on the edge of the bed again and looked into the man's steady eyes. "If it has to be, it has to be. Don't you think—"

Blanding took four steps forward, and stretched out his right hand.

The Toff let him grip his coat, then, almost lazily, moved his right hand and gripped the older man's wrist. He did not appear to do so tightly, but the strength went out of the man's arm, the strong fingers loosened their hold.

"I'm serious," Rollison said. "We must talk."

He thought that Blanding might try to fight, even considered the possibility of his telling the maid to telephone for the police. He stared into Blanding's narrowed eyes, seeing a little vein swelling in the man's neck, and getting larger; a pulse in Blanding's temple was beating, the vein blue against the redness of his skin.

Georgina sobbed, deep, wracking sobs, the only sound in the room.

Then, slowly:

"Go downstairs," said Blanding. "I'll join you there in five minutes."

"No," said Rollison. "No consultation with Georgina first."

"Damn your insolence!" roared Blanding. He tried to snatch his hand away, failed, then swept his other hand towards Rollison's face; Rollison pushed it away with an almost careless ease, and then stood up; he moved Blanding from him, and the man staggered.

"Are you coming?" Rollison demanded.

Blanding did not once look away from him until, after a long period of silence between them, he looked at Georgina. Her sobbing had quietened, although her shoulders still shook, and she did not look up.

Blanding turned to the maid.

"Stay with Miss Georgina," he ordered, and then moved towards the door. Guessing something of the anger raging in him, and giving him full marks for his iron composure, Rollison reached the door at the same time as Blanding. They walked side by side along the passage and down the stairs.

Moor was standing bewilderedly at the drawing-room door.

Blanding ignored him, and Rollison gave him a smile which was a warning not to join them. Blanding led the way to another room; taking a key-ring from his pocket he unlocked the door of a square study, lined almost to the ceiling with books in glass-fronted cases. There was an atmosphere of snug opulence about the room; the walnut desk glistened beneath the desk-lamp which went on from a switch by the door; and everything seemed new.

Blanding closed the door, but did not sit down.

"Well?"

Rollison took out his cigarette case.

"I'm sorry about this," he said. "I was afraid that if I went we might lose precious time."

"As far as I am concerned you are talking nonsense," said Blanding, ignoring the case. "Say what you have to say, and get out."

Rollison shrugged.

"If you're going to keep it up, I can't help either you or Georgina."

"I was not aware that we needed help."

"Weren't you?" Rollison lit a cigarette and dropped the match into an ashtray. "Georgina knows she does, but she's afraid of asking for it. Afraid is an ugly word."

"If you are trying to make me think——" began Blanding.

"Great Scott, no!" exclaimed Rollison. "You can't make men think; if they won't do it themselves you might as well give up trying."

Blanding's face took on a deeper shade of red.

"Your manner is quite offensive."

"I know," said Rollison. "I'm sorry. I think Georgina is in acute danger, and I want to help her. I don't think you realize it, and I don't think she does."

"I think you are talking nonsense!"

"I may be," admitted Rollison. He drew deeply on his

101

cigarette, then stepped across the room and sat on the corner of the desk. Blanding did not move. Two leather arm-chairs, with well-filled cushions, stood on either side of a red brick fireplace, a reading lamp and a book-rest near one of them; a book was lying open upon it. Rollison saw the title at the head of a page: *The Faith That Must Offend*. He narrowed his eyes and looked more earnestly at Blanding.

"Yes, I may be," he continued, "but this afternoon I saw a woman, rather older than Georgina, but as attractive in her way. She had been strangled."

"What the devil are you talking about?" demanded Blanding.

'I've shaken him,' thought Rollison, and felt more hopeful. "What I saw this afternoon," he said aloud. "The woman who was murdered was frightened—as Georgina is frightened now—and there is some reason for thinking that the same people caused the fear in each case. I can't be sure. Incidentally, the police know all about it."

Blanding relaxed, stepped to his desk and selected, with great care, a cigar from a silver box. Then he said:

"Will you have one of these? A drink?"

"No, thanks," said Rollison, surprised at Blanding's changed manner. "Seriously, Blanding, I'm sorry about the incident upstairs. If I hadn't felt that it was urgent I shouldn't have forced myself into 'Gina's room, and I certainly wouldn't have had a trial of strength with you."

"If you're serious, and there's anything in what you say, that doesn't matter," said Blanding, testily. "I can hardly believe that you're right. My daughter"—he made the word emphatic, as if to make sure that Rollison understood that he regarded Georgina as his real daughter, not one by marriage—"has had a severe shock." He broke off when Rollison smiled faintly, and for the first time a glimmer of a smile showed in his own eyes. "Yes, I do know you! I was saying, Georgina had an extremely severe shock this morning."

"What was it?" asked Rollison.

"A close friend of hers was involved in a road crash

yesterday. You may know him—Teddy Marchant. He—but, of course, Rollison! You figured prominently in the Marchant Trust case, didn't you?"

Rollison said, swiftly: "Yes." The news was a sharp blow, for he had been very fond of Teddy Marchant; but he forced himself not to think too deeply about it then, and added: "Was Georgina as fond of Teddy as all that?"

"I think she was. She is—" Blanding hesitated, and then said resignedly: "Well, she is a little inconsistent, but I had hoped that she and Marchant—" he broke off, while Rollison thought of Bob Moor's hopeful 'practically engaged'. "However, the point is that Georgina was very much affected by the news, which reached her before lunch."

"Yes?" said Rollison.

"And I think it is the reason for her breakdown," went on Blanding. "She has been very jumpy all day, but forced herself to remain at her work. She is—" he paused —"very highly strung, Rollison."

"Yes," repeated Rollison.

"Is that all you can say?" demanded the older man.

"I'm trying to fit everything in its place," Rollison said. "Not easy. Not—" he paused "—normal for Georgina."

"As I say, she is highly strung."

"Ye-es," said Rollison again, and then smiled quickly, almost nervously. "Is it just nerves? Has she always been quite so jumpy? Or have you noticed it more in the past few weeks or months?"

"I think she had been more serious about Marchant, and the fact that he has been on operational duty has affected her," said Blanding, stiffly.

"It could be, but—she *has* been more jumpy lately?"

"She has."

"Could there be something else, too?"

Blanding said: "Exactly what do you mean?"

Rollison eyed him evenly, and then said, in a slow, measured voice:

"If I were to follow my inclination I'd ask you to get a

doctor to examine her, and then go by what he says," he said. "But you can face it. I think she may have been taking drugs."

Blanding snapped: "What's that? Georgina! Rollison, if I thought you were serious—"

"I know, I know," said Rollison hastily. "You would knock my head off. Blanding, why should I express an opinion like that for the sake of it? If it's true, then she's not far gone and you'll be able to pull her round with proper treatment. If I'm wrong—well, no harm is done."

"I think the suggestion is positively slanderous!"

"Will you call a doctor?"

After a prolonged pause, in which neither man's eyes dropped, Blanding snapped his fingers and said:

"Oh, I suppose I'd better; I won't be satisfied until I know that you are talking nonsense."

"That's fine," murmured Rollison. "I hope I am, but—" he shrugged. "Can you get him here to-night?"

"I certainly don't propose to waste time," said Blanding. He looked towards the telephone, and then, his hand stretching out towards it, added: "But you didn't come to see whether Georgina was taking drugs. What did you want from her?"

"I wanted to find out whether she knows anything about a man named Charmion," said the Toff, almost casually. Then he stared, his eyes widening in amazement, at the transformation in Blanding; he had never seen more fury in a man's eyes.

CHAPTER XIII

THE TOFF KEEPS
HIS OWN COUNSEL

Before then, Blanding had looked as if he would strike the Toff, and his anger had been clear although controlled; now it made him like a man possessed. His whole expression changed, his voice was thick, he strode to Rollison and gripped his arms. Rollison could feel his fingers trembling.

"What the devil do you mean? What has Charmion to do with it? If you don't speak at once, I'll—"

Rollison made no effort to release himself.

"A Charmion is in it," he said, "but I don't know how, and I don't know which one. I had an appointment with 'Gina this morning and before I arrived she had been given a card with the one word 'Charmion,' in ink which faded. One Charmion and I have not been friends in the past, and I thought it was a crack at me. It might have been the reason for Georgina's manner to-day—not the fact that Marchant was hurt."

Blanding growled: "Is that the truth?"

"Of course it is," said Rollison, and then, gently, released his arms; they hurt where Blanding had gripped them. "What do you know of Charmion?"

He wondered what the reaction would be if he told Blanding that Charmion had seen Georgina, who had left him promising to do what she could. He wondered, too, what made Blanding fly into so wild a fury.

"And that's all?"

"That's all."

Blanding said: "If I thought that man was worrying Georgina I would—" he broke off. "Damn you, Rollison, you've upset me more than I've been upset in years!"

"Not I," said Rollison. "Blame the facts, not me."

"I'm not so sure," said Blanding. He stepped to the telephone, referring to a pad of numbers before dialling one. He did not speak until the receiver crackled, then: "Is Dr. Race there, please? . . . Sir Roland Blanding . . ." he waited without looking at the Toff, and when the receiver crackled again went on: "Race? Blanding here. Can you come over at once? . . . To see Georgina . . . I'm not sure, but I'm worried . . . Good. I'll see you in half an hour." The inflection of his voice did not alter, and when he replaced the receiver he looked at Rollison and then at his cigar, which had gone out. He struck a match and drew on the cigar. "He'll be here quite soon. We'll know then."

"Good!" said Rollison. "Meanwhile—what of Charmion?"

"I have no desire to hear the name mentioned," said Blanding slowly.

"Now, come," reasoned Rollison, "if Charmion—one or the other of them—is behind this, he may have been responsible for supplying drugs to Georgina."

Blanding said, in a tone of horror:

"*What* did you say?"

"Need I repeat it?" asked Rollison.

Blanding stood staring at him and in the man's eyes there was an expression akin to that in Georgina's earlier in the evening. It made Rollison wonder whether this man would talk freely or whether he would take refuge in a silence which would only serve to worsen the situation.

Rollison spoke after a long pause.

"What *do* you know of Charmion?" he asked mildly.

Blanding said: "I would like to see the man in hell!" He said 'hell' as if he meant it; it was no mere figure of speech. That, and the title of the opened book on the rest, told Rollison something of this man; he was earnest and sincere, and he believed in eternal damnation; so, for that matter, did Rollison.

"How long have you known him?" Rollison asked.

"Three years too long," said Blanding.

"You mean just three years?" Rollison's heart leapt and he felt a keen anxiety, greater than any since he had entered this house.

"I mean three years almost to the day," said Blanding. "And he . . ."

He did not stop for the next fifteen minutes, unfolding a story which made Rollison realize much of what he felt. Rollison sympathized with him, although there were moments when he thought Blanding had read more into it than there was. It was a strange story, almost bizarre; but it was told with a vehement earnestness which made it obvious that Blanding felt deeply.

The point which mattered most, to Rollison, was that he hated Charmion's brother.

Rollison walked from Portman Place to Gresham Terrace.

It was now raining steadily, as if it did not mean to leave off before the streets were running with water and the earth was saturated. It was a cold rain, too, and Rollison buttoned up his macintosh and walked through it, deep in thought and only aware of the elements when, at the corners, he turned into the wind.

Charmion's brother, he thought; and Anderson, if he had told the truth to the first Charmion, had seen the man's wife.

He wondered whether Anderson had called at the flat.

He hoped that the man would not be waiting for him, for he needed time to try to get his thoughts in order and to separate the chaff from the plentiful wheat. Slowly but surely, a story was building itself out of the mass of relevant and irrelevant detail; there was the hitherto unexpected existence of the three people in whom Charmion had placed his trust; and there was Blanding's evidence, now, that the younger Charmion was a rogue.

There was no more, perhaps, than that.

A man of Blanding's convictions would feel it more strongly than most, perhaps, although any man, whether of faith or not, would feel it strongly enough. It was very simple; the younger Charmion had pretended to be in

107

love with Blanding's own daughter—who was now in the nursing service. There had been a child, a promise to marry—and then the discovery that the man was already married.

An ordinary story; yet a bizarre touch was in the fact that right until the last moment, and even now, Blanding's daughter believed in Charmion, and did not hink that he had betrayed her. It was there, also, in Blanding's hatred for him. The tragedy had been made better or worse, according to the point of view, by the death of the child in early infancy.

Blanding had thought it a closed chapter until tonight.

Rollison reached the flat, and Grice's man went off to telephone his chief.

There was a light beneath the door, which meant that someone of whom Jolly did not wholly approve was waiting in the entrance hall. Rollison opened the door with his key, and Anderson rose from a chair his expression, for so cynical and experienced a man, surprisingly eager. But, it was not so eager as that of Bob Moor, who rose quickly from the same settee. With a sense of shock, Rollison realized that he had fogotten the youngster.

"Rollison—" began Anderson.

"Mr. Rollison!" exclaimed Moor.

"Could it be one at a time?" asked Rollison.

"But—" began Anderson.

"How is she?" cried Moor. "Mr. Rollison, I don't think—"

"She's quite all right," Rollison assured him. "She's had a shock, but she'll get over it. She didn't tell you anything that you haven't told me, did she?"

Anderson, taking his cue, stood back and lit a cigarette; but he gave an impression of suppressed anxiety and eagerness which titillated Rollison's curiosity.

"That's one of the things I wanted to see you about," said Moor eagerly. "I forgot at the time. Mr. Rollison, she told me about a man who frightened her—apparently she saw him this morning and again this evening. She thought he was following her. She even made me go to the window and look out, in spite of the black-out. She said it was a man with a face like a parrot. There was no one there, of course, but I thought you ought to know."

Rollison's expression was bland.

"I'm glad you remembered it," he said.

"But what can I do?" demanded Moor. "I've only three more days left in London, and—oh, I know I can't expect you to be interested, but I feel the very devil about it. She's a different girl! Why, the last time I was on leave—"

"She's not been well," said Rollison, gently. "It's only just been realized. Don't worry about her. If you'd like to, give me a ring in the morning, about ten o-clock. Will you?"

"Why, yes," said Moor, promptly. "You—you're sure it's nothing else?"

"What else should it be?" demanded Rollison.

"Well, this little fellow, and her hysterics, and—" Moor broke off. "I suppose I'm imagining things. Look here, Rollison—" he dropped the 'Mr.' for the first time, showing the intensity of his feelings. "You're not just stalling me? There isn't anything the matter? If I thought I could help—" he broke off, miserably.

"You may be able to, later," said Rollison reassuringly. "When 'Gina's convalescent, shall we say?" There was a cheerful gleam in his eyes, a man-to-man note in his voice; they worked miracles, for Moor seemed to be much happier on the instant. He said "Thanks" warmly, and then nodded to Anderson a little awkwardly. Rollison saw him to the head of the stairs, and Moor walked down cautiously, for he had no torch and would not borrow one of the Toff's.

In the hall, Anderson was standing up, and he spoke quickly as Rollison closed the door.

"Who's that, Rolly?"

"One of Georgina Scott's young men."

"I thought as much." The light remained in Anderson's eyes, and Rollison was amazed, for he had imagined that nothing could excite Anderson.

109

The man's face was leathery, his nose, cheeks and eyes gave evidence of heavy drinking; at one time he had been good-looking, but age and drink had spoiled that, although he still looked presentable. His careless dress did not improve him, and his moustache was thick but badly trimmed, one side much longer than the other. Had Rollison been asked to sum up Anderson in a few words, he would have said that he was an able, cynical, unimpressionable soak; but the eagerness in his eyes qualified 'cynical.' "I thought as much," repeated Anderson. "I thought I recognized her at Charmion's flat."

"For what you didn't do there, thanks," said Rollison.

Anderson waved a hand. "I thought you'd want to be after the girl. Rollison, this is about the biggest thing I've met in years!"

"It's big, yes," said Rollison.

"Man, it's colossal! And I thought—" Anderson shrugged whatever he thought away. "I checked up on those three people, Rolly. They weren't at the addresses you gave me, but Charmion's wife lived not far away. It's absolutely astonishing!"

"What is?" asked Rollison, trying not to be impatient.

"She's just a hag!" exclaimed Anderson. "She couldn't ever have been much more. *Charmion's* wife. The flat's a dream—no shortage of money, that's certain, but the woman's sixty if she's a day."

"Oh," said Rollison, absurdly.

"She's absolutely raddled," said Anderson. "Dope! I thought I knew what the damned stuff did, but I've never seen anyone eaten up with it like Mrs. Charmion. It turned me, and I've seen some things one way and the other." He waved his hand again as if he wanted to get the memory of Charmion's wife out of his mind. "The others—the brother and his wife—"

"Did you find them?" demanded Rollison, sharply.

"They're on the stage," said Anderson. "They do a song and dance act. They've a flat in Queen's Gate, plenty of money, but—when I arrived they nearly jumped out of their skins. How do you manage it?"

"Manage what?" demanded Rollison, not surprised at that startling question; it was almost as though he were incapable of feeling surprise; new statements, new discoveries just piled on to those disclosed and added to the turgid mass.

"Don't keep that up," said Anderson. "They're so scared that they jump in unison; you've managed them all right!"

"I didn't know of their existence until an hour or two before I saw you at Mile End," said Rollison. "I haven't seen them or worked on them. They're complete strangers to me."

Anderson's blood-shot eyes widened and he said weakly:

"Don't try to fool me, Rolly."

"I'm not."

"But—" Anderson looked positively dazed. "What's scared them, then? I—no, I don't believe you! I dropped your name into the conversation almost casually, and they turned sea-green."

"Oh," said Rollison. "Then it must have been telepathy."

"Are you serious?"

"Very serious."

"But they *are* scared of you."

"Someone else has made them so; we'll have to find out how it was done. We might find it useful in future," added the Toff, bleakly, "—if there's any future. I like this less and less. But what led you to such extravagance?"

"What extravagance?"

"You said it was the biggest thing for years," Rollison reminded him.

Anderson said: "Look here, Rollison, you must know more about this than you pretend—it's no use coming over all innocent Charmion's out of jail. He left his money in the hands of his relatives. His wife, who had the major influence, is so raddled with drugs that she would sign anything put to her. The brother and his wife

111

have conspired with someone—you probably know who!
—to get Charmion's money. Well, they've succeeded. It's
gone to build up—"

"Oh, damn!" exclaimed Rollison, for across Anderson's
words the telephone rang and, almost at the same moment, the front-door bell made him start; it was a battery
one, with the bell fitted to the back of the door.

Anderson, interrupted at the moment of exciting dis-
closures, looked from one bell to the other, and Jolly
came hurrying into the hall.

"Shall I answer the door, sir?" asked Jolly.

"No, the 'phone," said Rollison. He stepped to the
door himself and opened it, keeping a little to one side
and wondering whether he were too jitery. He did not
see who was there; he did not see a thing until two stabs
of yellow flame appeared and two sharp, sneezing
sounds followed—and, close upon them, there came a
gasp from Anderson.

CHAPTER XIV

THE SECOND ATTEMPT

Rollison stood quite still.

For a split second he did not know whether to go after the man who had fired the shots or whether to hurry to Anderson; but he was not undecided for long. He took his own gun from his pocket and pulled the door wider open, firing once; but in the light from the open door he could see only the top of a trilby hat, disappearing down the stairs. He jumped forward, and his foot kicked against a string which was stretched across the landing from wall to wall. He sprawled, saving himself from falling by grabbing at the banisters; as he went, he heard groaning in the flat, and the clattering of footsteps below. The echoes of his own shot rang about the landing, the only loud noise that there had been.

Downstairs, a door opened, another banged. He thought he heard people running.

"Rol—Rollison," called Anderson. There was a taut, strange note in his voice. "Rollison—a man named Guy. Guy!" Rollison could hear his hoarse, laboured breathing, while someone called gruffly up the stairs:

"What's the matter up there?"

"It's all right," called Rollison. He stepped through into the hall and heard Jolly speaking into the telephone.

"Yes, this very moment—Mr. Anderson, of the *Echo* . . . Very good, Mr. Grice." Jolly replaced the receiver and said: "That was Superintendent Grice, sir; he's coming right away. He had no time to tell me what he rang up about."

"Rol—Rollison," gasped Anderson, from the floor.

He had not been there for more than thirty seconds; it had all happened with a speed so bewildering that it did not seem real. Now Jolly hurried into the bathroom, needing no telling what to get, and Rollison was on one knee beside the reporter, whose face was distorted and whose breathing was so harsh that it was like a file grating upon metal.

"I—just saw him," Anderson gasped. "Guy—little man —that mask—"

"Don't talk," said Rollison, resting the man against his arm and exploring his breast with his right hand; he felt the warm blood from the wounds; they were on the left side, and although the bullets had missed the heart they had pierced the lung. "Don't talk," repeated Rollison. "You'll be—"

"Guy" gasped Anderson. "Guy. Rollison! You remember—Charmion's—League. Charmion's League—"

"Yes, but don't—"

"Child's play," said Anderson and choked. His body heaved. "My God, how it hurts! Child's play—Rollison. Nothing on—"

He put out his right hand and gripped Rollison's shoulder; Rollison could feel the pressure of his fingers getting more and more tense; Anderson was holding on, trying to save himself from dying, although he must have known, as Rollison did, that there was little hope.

He kept his eyes open and his teeth clenched. Rollison said: "Take it easy, Mike," and then Jolly came hurrying into the hall, carrying a bowl of water and a towel. But before he had put them on the floor, Anderson's eyes widened and there was a choking noise in the back of his throat.

He muttered something; it might have been 'Guy'. And then he died.

Rollison straightened up from the reporter's body and looked at Jolly; but he did not really see his man. He lived through the whole incident, from the moment when the two bells had rung, and thought of the bitterly ironic fact that Grice had called at the same time as a murderer.

Had Anderson really seen the man; and had it been Guy?

He had been standing in front of the door as it had opened, refusing to move; and so he had had a better chance than either Rollison or Jolly to see who had stood there with the gun. There were no grounds for thinking that the reporter had been mistaken, except the fact that the light had been poor.

Everything in the affair was perfectly done, except—

"The little things," said Rollison, *sotto voce*. "The little unexpected things, but then—" he shrugged "—can they be perfect?" He was wondering whether the flaws were accidental or deliberate. For anyone to have paid off his cabby at the restaurant had been foolish; the man should have been allowed to wait and then go off, disgruntled, to report to the police that he had been bilked. Yet after the tortuous plan to enmesh him in a charge of murder and assault, they had paid the cabby off and so given Rollison the opportunity to prove his story.

Jolly interrupted his reverie, saying:

"Should I telephone a doctor, sir?"

"No," said Rollison. "Grice will arrange all that, I think—you told him just what had happened?" Jolly nodded. "Then that's all right. What ought we to look for in the way of clues?" There was no humour in his smile, for although he had seen death by violence a hundred times, the suddenness of Anderson's death affected him as much as the fact that the man had died on the point of a great disclosure.

There again they had failed—'they' meaning the murderers. Not one man only, that was certain; it was an organization, a syndicate, its members frightened in some ways and acting like this because of their fear. That seemed the reasonable explanation, and yet it did not explain the confidence with which they acted.

Anderson had robbed them of full success. His last, hardly coherent words had told of something to make the first Charmion's League of Physical Beauty negligible and laughable—'child's play,' Anderson had said. His excitement, the astonishing eagerness he had betrayed, surely proved that he had made a discovery of enormous importance.

"It hardly matters," said Rollison, aloud. "What's that, Jolly?"

"Have you examined what tripped you up?" asked Jolly.

"No, not yet. The neighbours are very good to-night, aren't they?" Rollison had expected callers after the shooting, but his shout to the single inquirer seemed to have satisfied the other tenants. "Switch on the landing light."

The landing light was subdued, shining about a plain, square space, with rubber on the floor and newly distempered walls. The staircase and wainscoting were of wood; Rollison examined the latter near the stairs, soon seeing the piece of cord, the second over which he had tripped. It was fastened at one side by a small nail, but had pulled free at the other. It was not likely that they had been careless enough to leave their finger-prints on the woodwork, and in any case Grice could check.

Then Rollison saw the gun, in one corner; it made a strange shadow on the floor immediately beyond it—like a man's crooked finger and closed palm. It was a small automatic, very like his own.

"Of course it is," said Rollison as he bent down to pick it up. "They all look alike." But he did not touch it until he had taken a handkerchief from his pocket, and then, after making sure that there was nothing else of interest on the landing,. and after putting the piece of cord on one side, so that Grice could not trip up, he returned to the flat.

Jolly had not moved Anderson, although he had brought a sheet and spread it over the reporter's body.

"One gun." Rollison's voice sounded strained. "Familiar, Jolly?" He was examining the butt, and Jolly looked at him without speaking. "Familiar!" repeated Rollison, his voice sharp. "It's mine!"

Jolly said nothing, but just stared.

"Mine!" repeated Rollison. "My initials, my notches—the gun I had with me this afternoon, and I thought—" He took the other automatic from his pocket and examined it; it was exactly the same, except that the initials 'R.R.' had not been engraved, there were no other marks. He drew a deep breath as he put them both on the table. "So they stole it, and planned to leave it here for the police of find. My gun—my bullets. Who killed Anderson?"

"It is certainly clever, sir." Jolly's voice was like a gargantuan sigh. "Will you—" he paused.

"Tell Grice?" Rollison barked. "Yes, of course I shall, or they'll send him a post card to tell him to examine the gun more closely, and to examine mine. The swine, they—" he broke off. "Jolly, I'm not so good as I was. This case is getting on my nerves."

"Which is exactly what they want, sir," said Jolly.

"Ye-es." Rollison shrugged. "Well, we can't do any more until Grice and his men arrive. Did you hear what Anderson said?"

"I caught a little of it, but I was not near the door all the time, sir. The other young man—"

"A Mr. Robert Moor, who is in love with Georgina Scott," said Rollison, and promptly forgot about Moor. "*Guy*, Jolly, the man who's been everywhere, that's our *bête noire*. I wonder how long your Lauriston fellow will be with his identification of that mask? If we can find out who made it, we might get somewhere."

"I think I told you, sir, that he hoped to have some information by to-morrow morning," said Jolly. "Did I understand you to say that Miss Scott is ill?"

Rollison told him a little of what he knew, deciding to tell the story in detail when Grice arrived. It was obvious that he must keep the police informed of every step; if he kept anything to himself it would probably be precisely that they wanted. As it was, this second murder would surely force Grice's hand; how could the police allow him to remain free?

He did not know that Grice was waiting outside the house for another police-car carrying a police-surgeon and two sergeants, and talking to a tall, slim man who was breathing heavily. The man's name was Simonds; he was one of the two whom Grice had detailed to watch the Toff.

Grice was brusque, and Simonds, drawing in deep breaths, was worried and apologetic.

"I kept outside, sir, and Wilson was at the back. I saw a little man enter, and I thought I'd better follow him upstairs—I'd already let Anderson go up. I heard talking, sir, and there was just enough light for me to see the little man bending down by the wainscoting. I—I thought I would wait a bit, and stop him coming down. Then the little man rang the bell. I was on the landing below, sir. The light came from Rollison's flat—I just saw Rollison —and then the caller fired." Simonds paused, but went on when Grice did not speak. "I was going forward to stop him as he ran downstairs, but I slipped, I didn't lose much time, sir, but went after him pretty fast, but he got away. I—I'm terribly sorry, sir."

Grice nodded, but said nothing; miserably, Simonds waited when the other car arrived and the party went upstairs; he knew that he had put up a very poor show; he did not know that he had saved the Toff from much unpleasantness.

On the arrival of the police party at the flat, the telephone rang, and Rollison answered it, indicating Anderson's body and, with a gesture, giving Grice permission to go where he pleased. Then he said: "Hallo?" and was surprised to hear a deep and familiar voice.

"Rollison?" Sir Roland Blanding asked, abruptly.

"Yes."

"You were right," said Blanding; the words seemed to make the wires sing a tense and emotional song. "She has been taking drugs. Cocaine, my doctor thinks."

"Ye-es," said Rollison, slowly. "I'm sorry."

"That's not good enough! Where did she get them?"

"We have to find that out," said Rollison, "and we aren't going to let the grass grow under our feet. Bland-

118

ing, keep her in her room and make quite sure that she doesn't leave the house until I've seen you again."

"She isn't likely to be ill enough to be confined to her room," said Blanding; his real strength, it seemed, was pertinacity; Rollison considered it obstinacy.

"Make out that she is," said Rollison. "Better to have her in screaming hysterics because she can't get out than to walk into more trouble. I can't stop now, but you'll be well-advised to keep her in. Good-bye."

He rang off without giving Blanding a chance to reply, then turned to look at Grice and the police-surgeon, a grey-haired little man with a berry-red face and *pince-nez* which was near the end of his nose; Dr. Lefroy, whom Rollison knew well. As they examined Anderson more police arrived, including the finger-print men and photographer. They swarmed about the flat, with flashlights snapping and hissing and powder being spread here and there, determined to do their job thoroughly and, Rollison thought, mainly because Grice would have to make a full report, and produce evidence that he had left nothing undone against him.

There followed a period of inactivity which Rollison found trying; there seemed something ominous in it. Grice's silence seemed to hold a menace; from time to time he looked at the guns on the table and wondered whether he would be wise to tell the police exactly what had happened.

Grice looked up, at last, with a smile that made Rollison feel foolish.

"Our busy day, Rolly!" Grice straightened up and took out a cigarette case. "Jolly gave me the drift of the story, but—"

Rollison filled in all the details, including the discovery of his own gun, and a sergeant, a lean-faced man with a hungry look, took it down in shorthand. When it was finished the man read it back in a metallic voice which sounded as if Grice, by giving him the order, had put a coin in a slot-machine. When it was over, Grice said:

119

"Is that right, Rolly?"

"That's all," said Rollison.

"You're sure of the name 'Guy'?"

"I'm sure Anderson uttered it, yes, and I'm equally sure about the 'child's play.' Have you learned anything?"

"Nothing outstanding," said Grice. "Anderson"—he looked at the sheet over the man's body—"wasn't a man to exaggerate."

"He was brimming over with excitement," said Rollison. "How often do Press men get worked up?" Grice shrugged. "Rarely enough to make it remarkable."

"He didn't give you the Charmions' address?"

"He gave me part of it. They've a flat in Queen's Gate."

"May I use your phone?" asked Grice.

Rollison nodded, and Grice told the Yard man who answered him to make inquiries about the Charmions and to keep the Queen's Gate flat watched; he also gave instructions for the first Charmion to be watched, as well as his wife, Laura. Grice seemed to be on the telephone for a long time. He replaced it at last, and then said thoughtfully: "Where does Blanding come in on this?"

Rollison said: "It's nothing to do with Anderson's murder, and I don't want to make it official."

Grice said: "All right. My men will be done here in a few minutes." The police-surgeon, who was a notoriously silent man, had finished, so Grice had only to attend to the odds and ends, and to superintend the removal of Anderson's body. He told Rollison nothing of Simonds, but allowed him to understand that he was in no great trouble. The Toff was both relieved and mildly curious.

Then, in the study, with Jolly standing by the door, Rollison went into further detail about Georgina and Blanding, the young man named Moor, and all that had preceded hs return to the flat. He concluded:

"I've told Blanding nothing about Georgina's visit to

the man at Shaftesbury Avenue," he said. "I don't think it's necessary yet, do you?"

"No," conceded Grice. "Do you think there's any doubt about Blanding's story? Did he know the second Charmion or the first?"

"Oh, he knew the second," said Rollison. "His story was too categorical for him to have been telling a half-truth. Anyhow, you can find out about the daughter and the child, can't you?"

"Yes," said Grice, and then more crisply: "I wish I knew how the Charmion-Blanding contact originated. How is it that the older Charmion knows Georgina?"

"Answer that, and you'll answer nearly everything," said Rollison, unhelpfully. "She was too young to have been under his influence, yet his name frightened her. True, she might have been affected by the name, which would give any member of the family a nasty jolt, and that might explain why she was so jumpy after I saw her at the coffeeshop, but—" he shrugged. "This affected her pretty deeply. The drugs, diagnosed by one doctor, explain part of it, of course, but not all. 'Charmion' meant far more to her than she admitted." He shrugged his shoulders and took out cigarettes. "Will you have a drink?" he asked, belatedly, and when Grice refused, looked at Jolly. "Make some coffee, will you?" He sat in the chair at his desk, on which the stuffed carcase of the effigy remained, and added, a little wearily: "What do you think is the major factor now?"

Grice said: "What Anderson knew."

"And was he killed because of what he knew, or was it another attempt to put a rope round my neck?"

"I can't believe that you would be framed twice," Grice said, judicially. "And if the flat was watched, they'd know that Jolly was here and that there would be his evidence to support yours." He left it at that.

"If I weren't who I am, would you be satisfied with the evidence of a manservant in support of his employer?" demanded the Toff. "Of course you wouldn't! I doubt whether these people know that you're quite so loyal to me as you are. I think it's probable that Anderson was killed because of what he had learned, and the rest was put in for make-weight. Anderson died for the same reason as Hilda Brent."

"She knew what he knew," Grice mused.

"Yes." Rollison scowled. "Any word of Fifi or Joe?"

"Nothing at all."

"We are doing well," said Rollison, sarcastically. "Well, there's one thing that can be done, and I'd like to handle it myself." He paused, hopefully.

"What do you mean?" asked Grice.

"Charmion," said Rollison, "the first Charmion—and why he talked to Georgina."

Grice said: "Do you think you'll get anything out of him?"

"If he's genuine—and what he said to Anderson makes that seem likely—he's probably feeling better towards me than towards you. I am his friend in need!" Rollison smiled, mirthlessly. "Shall I try him?"

"Yes," said Grice, decisively. "You'll let me know what he says as soon as you've finished, won't you? When will you go?"

"Now," said Rollison. "Is it still raining?"

"It was when I arrived," Grice told him.

It was teeming when Rollison and the Superintendent reached the street. Grice's car was outside with a chauffeur, and he offered the Toff a lift; the Toff refused, not because he preferred to walk, but because he wanted to make reasonably sure that he was not being followed, and felt fairly certain that Grice had taken precautions, hence his extreme amiability. Then he remembered a factor of importance and, as the car moved off, its headlights making the rain look even heavier, he hurried in its wake, shouting. Grice heard the shouts and the car pulled up.

"Hallo?" asked Grice, winding the window down.

Rollison said: "Sergeant Wilson—any news?"

"Wilson—oh, after your man in the bowler hat."

122

Grice's face was in shadow, but Rollison caught a note of uncertainty in his voice. "No. Wilson lost him after following him about London for two hours. He went out to Golders Green and called at a block of flats. He wasn't there for more than ten minutes, and eventually Wilson lost him at Piccadilly Circus."

"And what about the flats?"

"I've done nothing yet," said Grice. "But I will."

So it was getting too fast and furious for Grice, as well as for him, he reflected as he walked in the wake of the car. He shrugged his shoulders, trying to dismiss all thought of the bowler-hatted man; he failed, for in spite of the darkness he could not rid himself of a feeling that he was being followed. Twice he stopped on the edge of the pavement, but the footsteps he thought he heard either stopped or were not there. He went on, listening intently, and paused again; he could not decide whether it were fancy or not.

In the lobby at the foot of the stairs of the building where Charmion lived he took off his macintosh. He shook the worst of the water from it, folded it inside out, and then hurried up the stairs. He thought of Anderson, who had once waited up there with such amirable discretion—and he thought, too, that he might be accredited with a motive for Anderson's murder; Anderson had been in a position to spread information about the murder of Hilda.

He heard voices, much louder than Charmion's and Georgina's had been, and stood waiting. They were men's voices, raised in anger; a third, a woman's, kept interrupting, in ineffectual protests.

CHAPTER XV

BROTHER OF CHARMION

Rollison tapped sharply at the door.

The shouting stopped, and the hush was complete until the woman said in a high-pitched voice:

"Someone's there!"

"I know, you fool," said Charmion.

There was no mistaking his voice, and Rollison imagined that it was Charmion who stepped forward, with heavy tread, and began to unlock the door. He took an unconscionable time over it, and when he had it unlocked he did not open it wide, but peered through an inch-wide gap.

"Who's there?"

"Rollison," said Rollison, quietly.

"*Rollison!*" gasped the woman. "No, no! He can't come in, he mustn't come in."

There was a sharp sound; Rollison thought that Charmion had slapped the woman's face. She gasped and he thought he heard her stagger away. Then Charmion opened the door wide and stood aside for Rollison to enter.

Standing against the wall, with a hand at her face and her eyes round pools of terror, was a woman of no more than twenty-four or -five; and in spite of the terror in her face she had real beauty. On the other side of the room was a man who might have been Charmion.

Rollison felt quite sure that it was the man whom he had seen at the window; and it was from that moment that he felt convinced that Charmion's brother was involved more deeply in this affair than it appeared. Now the man was looking as scared as the woman—presumably, his wife. But he was acting; Rollison felt quite sure about it. The very way in which he raised his hands, as if to fend off a physical assault, indicated that.

"Rollison!" he exclaimed.

"Be quiet!" snapped Charmion. "Mr. Rollison did not come here to talk to you. What is it you want, Rollison? You may ignore my brother."

"Gil, you can't do this!" exclaimed the younger man.

"Unless you keep quiet, I will show you that I can do a great deal more," said Charmion, with a savage intensity.

The younger man seemed to sag. His wife crept round the room towards him, and they stood together while Rollison eyed Charmion. It was like seeing the past and the present together.

"What do you want?" Charmion repeated. "I have been quarrelling—perhaps you overheard something of it."

"I did," said Rollison. "So you found them, did you?"

"I found them," said Charmion. "I received an anonymous note, telling me—"

Rollison snapped: "Anonymous?"

"That is what I said," said Charmion; he had himself under better control than at Rollison's flat, as if this encounter with his relatives had given him a new confidence. "Why? Do you doubt that?"

"Did Anderson tell you?"

"I asked him whether he knew where to find them, but he said that he did not. I have little doubt that he lied— all newspaper reporters are liars; it is in their blood. No, I had an anonymous letter, Rollison, and I went to see them." Charmion looked dispassionately at his brother and the girl, whose terror had not diminished.

Rollison said: "What did Anderson come to tell you about?"

"My wife," said Charmion, very softly. "My wife and these two unspeakable swine."

"You're wrong, Gil!" cried Charmion's brother. "We knew nothing about it, I tell you; she insisted, she had her own way! We haven't seen her for a year!"

"I don't believe you," said Charmion.

"But it's true, I tell you. Rollison!" the man was perspiring freely; he used mascara, which was running, and rouge, which made him look like a doll—a sinister doll. "He thinks that we robbed him, but it's not true! Make him realize that it's not true!"

"That should be easy," said Rollison, sardonically.

"They have been trying to convince me that their incredible story is not a tissue of lies," said Charmion. "They expect me to believe that soon after I left, Laura —my wife—began to take drugs, and fell into the hands of unknown men, who made her sign away my wealth. They say that they were frightened. The truth is that they were party to it. The time will come when I will make them rue the day."

"We knew nothing about it!" The woman spoke, finding courage for the first time and stepping forward, both hands raised, looking at Charmion; Rollison deliberately effaced himself; it looked as if the quarrel would start afresh and he desired nothing more. "Laura told us that she wanted nothing more to do with us. We tried to reason with her, but—" she stopped again, and turned away; had she been anyone he knew, Rollison would have felt sorry for her, so great was her fear and her distress.

Charmion turned to Rollison.

"The lies pour out of them," he said.

"I shouldn't be surprised," said Rollison, "Am I in this? I mean, if you want an opinion on their truthfulness, I can't very well give it without knowing what they've said."

Charmion shrugged his shoulders and his brother exclaimed:

"Rollison, you've made life hell for us, but—but convince him we're telling the truth! We looked after everything perfectly, everything went smoothly, we made money for him—and then his wife got mixed up with Guy and the others." The man drew in a sharp, searing breath, as if waiting to see his reaction to the name 'Guy'.

Rollison remained impassive, and young Charmion went on: "It was hopeless from the start! He gave her drugs and we couldn't make her stop taking them. We even consulted a doctor, but she wouldn't undergo his treatment. We—we told Gilbert things were all right, we didn't want to upset him, but he came out before we expected him. We were working on the halls, trying to get a bit of something for him when he came home, we knew what a shock it would be!"

"Yes," said Charmion, softly—with the softness of a snake. "I came out too soon, there is no doubt of that. The rest"—he sneered—"lies, from beginning to end."

"Whom did you say his wife met?" asked Rollison.

"A man named Guy," gasped Charmion's brother. "A little man with a face like a bird. He could turn her round his little finger; she signed everything away to him."

"A face like a bird's," mused Rollison.

"The voice of a Judas," said Charmion, still softly.

"It's no use, Charles," said the woman; her voice surprised them all, for she had it under better control and had regained her composure. While they had not been looking at her she had powdered her face and even touched up her lips. "We'd better go. They won't believe us."

Rollison said slowly: "We might, in time. Why are you so frightened of me, Mrs. Charmion?"

She said: "Oh, don't make it worse! You know as well as we do."

"Are you going to turn the screw?" demanded Charles Charmion, tersely. "What about those letters?"

"And 'phone calls?" interpolated his wife.

"The visiting-cards," said Charmion's brother.

"And telegrams," said his wife.

Rollison looked from one to the other, and then said, mildly; "I know nothing about them. Have you any of them with you?"

"Oh, what's the use?" demanded Charmion's brother harshly. "Gil, don't trust him! Heaven knows *you* ought to know better than to trust him an inch! He's told us all the time that when you came out there would be the devil to pay; he's threatened and badgered us for a year now. Yes," he snapped at the Toff, "I've one of your cards here!" He put a trembling hand to his pocket, drew out a wallet, and extracted several cards. He sorted through them feverishly, then selected one and held it out to Rollison. "Well? Isn't that yours?"

Rollison took it, and Charmion looked at it.

It had Rollison's name printed on one side, with the Gresham Terrace address. On the reverse side was a pencilled drawing of a monocle, a top-hat, and a cane. The Toff often used such cards. They created a certain unnerving effect when delivered at the right moment, although not so great as he had once imagined.

"Well?" screeched Charles.

Rollison took out his own wallet, went through the same procedure as the man, and put one of his own cards next to that he had been given; there was a noticeable difference in the printing, the copper-plate engraving on the genuine card was smaller than on the other. On the reverse side were the sketches; they too were smaller and much neater.

"Not mine."

"Not—yours!" gasped Mrs. Charmion. "Then who—"

"One day, we'll know," said Rollison. He felt cold and tense. Each page turned in the story had its own absurdities, its own tortuous cunning. "If I were you," he advised Charmion, "I should give this pair the benefit of the doubt for the time being."

"Do you think I'm such a credulous fool?" demanded Charmion. "Do you expect me to believe that someone I don't know has set himself to get my money, to drug my wife until she is hardly sane, to frame my brother *and*"— he sneered—"to frame you at the same time? No, Rollison, *I* am not deceived."

He had created an even tenser atmosphere by the coldness of his voice. His brother and the woman hung on his words, the woman tight-lipped and still afraid, the man with his mouth agape, until into the silence there came a knock on the door, soft and timid. Yet it was enough to make them all start, and Rollison turned quickly.

The knock was repeated.

Charmion stepped towards the door and opened it, his movements brisk and decisive, reflecting his new-found confidence. Someone—a woman in a streaming cape—stood on the threshold, and Charmion said:

"Yes?"

A voice that was high-pitched with emotion answered him, one which made Rollison move swiftly towards the door.

"Please," the woman said. "I come, please, to see—" she gulped—"M'sieu Charmion! I am asked to come, this ees the address. My name ees Link, m'sieu, Fifi Link." She gulped again as if she could not bring herself to utter the words. "Please, ees M'sieu Charmion 'ere? I must see 'im."

Charmion stood aside, and Rollison stepped into Fifi's view. She stared at him, wide-eyed; her cheeks sagged, she looked a different woman from what she had been the night before. But a new light sprang to her eyes when she saw Rollison and she jumped forward, gripping his arm.

"M'sieu, M'sieu Roll'son! Please 'elp me, please make them return my Shoe, do not let them 'urt 'eem. Only for Shoe would I come to see that man who is so 'ateful!"

129

CHAPTER XVI

FIFI

If Charmion knew that she meant him, he gave no sign, but stepped farther away from the Frenchwoman and watched impassively as she gripped Rollison, shaking him, staring at him with her eyes streaming tears. She was so distraught that her words became unintelligible.

The others stood watching as the Toff tried to comfort her.

Swift, urgent thoughts passed through his mind. Where was Joe? Who had taken Joe from Fifi and, more important by far, who had sent Fifi here, naming Charmion as the man who could return her Joe?

Fifi grew quieter at last.

During the paroxysm, Charles Charmion and his wife had been edging towards the door, putting on their raincoats unostentatiously. As Rollison drew the Frenchwoman away from the door, Charles Charmion said in an agitated voice:

"You don't want us any more, Gil, do you?"

"Get out of here," said Charmion, soft-voiced. "If I ever have to see you again, I'll send for you." He waved them towards the door and his sister-in-law half ran towards it. But before they went out, Rollison said:

"Why the hurry, Charmion?"

"We're due to give a turn," said the younger Charmion. "If we don't get there on time we'll probably lose the engagement. Rollison, if you're sure you didn't send those messages—"

"Where is there a show so late as this?" demanded Rollison.

"It's a cabaret—"

"All right, where's the cabaret so late as this?" demanded Rollison, keeping an arm about Fifi's shoulders. She had quietened and was now looking up at the others, questions in her eyes; but she kept close to Rollison, as if taking comfort from his nearness.

"It's a private one," muttered the younger Charmion.

"Where?"

The man tried to bluster. "I don't see what it's got to do with you—"

"I shall want to see you afterwards," said Rollison, coldly.

"Oh, tell him, and let's get away," said Mrs. Charmion.

"It's at 1A, Littleton Place," said the younger Charmion, with poor grace, "at the corner of Port Street. Gil, don't forget that—"

Charmion said nothing, and his brother tightened his lips and turned away; yet Rollison could not rid himself of an impression that, as he turned, there was a grotesque smile on the dancer's face. The woman's expression did not alter. The door slammed behind them, and then their footsteps sounded as they hurried down the stairs; one of them stumbled. Young Charmion spoke, they appeared to recover and hurried down again.

Inside the flat it was very quiet.

Then Charmion stepped towards Fifi, who looked at him without recognition. Rollison thought that there was an expression which might have been pity and understanding in the man's eyes. Charmion stretched out a hand, scarred and calloused after his work on the moor, and rested it on Fifi's shoulder.

"Who sent you to me?" he asked.

Fifi stared: "You? *You* are Charmion?"

"I am," said Charmion.

"But—" Fifi began, and gasped. "The man who just went out now, 'e ees like ze Charmion I knew, yes. I did not dare to speak, M'sieu Roll'son, always I leave such things to you, but this—*this* ees not Charmion!"

"It is what they made me," Charmion said. "Why did you come?"

She turned to Rollison and said:

"M'sieu, I do not undairstand. This ees not the Charmion I 'ave thought of so much, no, eet ees a diff'rent man. But"—her eyes filled again with alarm—"where ees Shoe?"

"Who is Joe?" asked Charmion.

"Her husband," said Rollison, shortly, and then persuaded Fifi to tell her story.

She started slowly, with many comments and exclamations, but soon was in the swing of it; it was graphic because of the intensity of her feelings; her love for 'Shoe' was obvious in every word she uttered, every gleam in her dark eyes.

It had started early on the previous morning.

Joe had gone to the market but had not returned. A child had been sent to Fifi, with a note from him; it had told her to put up the 'Back Later' sign in the window and to join him at The Docker, a small public house not far away. Fifi had gone, expecting to find that Joe had met an old friend and wanted her to join in the reunion; it appeared that many of Fifi's French colony friends visited her from time to time.

Instead of Joe, she had been greeted by another message, obviously sent by Joe. She was to go to a house in Golders Green. Something in the way the note was delivered, rather than its actual words, had warned her of impending trouble. She had sent a messenger to the restaurant, to close it until she returned, and hurried to Golders Green. There the house had proved to be a vast block of mansion flats, and, when she had found the flat she wanted—Number 79, she said—she had been admitted and then told to wait if she wanted to see Joe again.

Listening to her story, Rollison sensed the same cold efficiency which planned every step perfectly; the arrangements were calculated to impress the excitable Fifi more than anything else could have done. 'A man' had convinced her that Joe was in danger and that to save him she would have to stay there. She had asked permission to send a message to the staff of the restaurant, but it

132

had been refused. She had been left alone for a long time, but, eventually 'the man' had returned; he had given her Charmion's name and the Shaftesbury Avenue address, and told her that Charmion knew where she could find Joe.

That was all.

"All the time, eet was Charmion," Fifi breathed, eyeing Charmion incredulously. "I knew that eet was Charmion, why else should I be so afraid? M'sieur"—she turned to Rollison again, her hands clenched—"where ees Shoe? All I ask is that you find 'eem an' return 'eem to me!"

Rollison looked at Charmion, and asked:

"Well, Charmion?"

"It is a fantastic story!" exclaimed Charmion. Something in his manner made Rollison thoughtful; he was too definite; suddenly, and for no reason at all, Rollison was reminded of Sir Roland Blanding. "I have no idea why she should be sent to me."

"But it must be Charmion!" cried Fifi.

"Can you explain this, Rollison?" Charmion asked, quietly. "I am completely at a loss."

"I'm beginning to believe that you might be," admitted Rollison. "Fifi, I'm looking for Joe now. I hope to find him before the night is out, but"—he paused, frowning—"you'd better not go back to Mile End just yet."

"But m'sieu—"

"I think you'd better go to my flat," said Rollison; and then more briskly: "I'll come with you soon." He looked at Charmion and went on: "Is there another room here?"

"Of course, there's my bedroom," said Charmion.

"Wait there, *chérie*," said Rollison, squeezing Fifi's shoulder reassuringly. His eyes were smiling, for he wanted Fifi more cheerful, and believed that he could raise her spirits. "I won't be long." He led her towards the door which Charmion opened and she went through.

Charmion closed the door and swung round.

"What do you know about this, Rollison?"

Rollison said: "Taking the facts as I know them, I should say that you're being framed, because—"

He told the story swiftly and concisely, glad that he could do so. It brought the revelant details clearer to his mind, helped him to assess the values of each item of information and all that had happened. He cut out all embellishments, and Charmion listened, hard-faced, twice restraining himself from interrupting only with an obvious effort.

Rollison finished, quietly:

"So, if we judge from that, we're both being framed. It would be helpful if we knew why."

"If anyone else had told me this story I would have refused to believe him," said Charmion, "but—" he broke off, then went on very gently: "I don't trust my brother. I think he left here feeling highly pleased with himself. He was always very fond of pulling fast ones. I think I shall go—"

Rollison said: "If you want to keep your feet dry, don't leave this apartment."

"That's absurd!" snapped Charmion. "I can go—"

"Anywhere you like," said Rollison, "but you'll probably wish you hadn't."

"Is that all you are going to say?"

"For the time being, yes," said Rollison, and smiled—there was a hint of gaiety in his expression which must have puzzled Charmion. "I think I can work the situation out if I'm left to myself."

"How can I be sure that you will consider my interests?" demanded Charmion.

"You have to trust to luck," said Rollison, lightly. "Fifi!" He raised his voice, and Fifi came so quickly that it was obvious she had been standing with a hand on the door. "We're going," he said. "I'll see you tomorrow, Charmion, but remember the advice for the night—stay put!"

Gripping Fifi's elbow, he hustled her to the door, opened it, and passed through with her. He closed the door with a bang, then stood for a moment, so that their eyes could get used to the gloom.

There was no movement behind him; even had there been the faint whistling would probably have prevented him from hearing it. He kept smiling until they reached the Avenue, and then, with the friendly darkness about him, hiding his face, he looked bleak and uncompromising. But there was a lilt in his voice as he chaffed Fifi and then shouted for a taxi; one drew near after they had walked nearly as far as the Circus.

Ten minutes later he was ushering Fifi into the flat, and saying to Jolly:

"You remember Mrs. Link, Jolly? She will be staying the night." Jolly bowed, and allowed himself to smile a greeting.

"But, of course, M'sieu Sholly!" exclaimed Fifi. "Always so sad! To Shoe, I 'ave said often, M'sieu Roll'son, 'e ees so sholly; M'sieu Sholly, 'e ees so sad!"

"Indeed," murmured Jolly.

Rollison said: "Fifi, I've one or two calls to make, but before I go I want you to think hard and find what you can remember. Ready?"

"I am prepared, m'sieu! I feel, now, that you weel find Shoe. That ees all that matters, and eef I can 'elp you—" she paused, eyeing him with bright eyes. "Proceed, m'sieu!"

"A child brought you the first message?"

"Yes, m'sieu."

"The second was telephoned to Bert Prior, at The Docker?"

"Yes, m'sieu."

"You went to 79, Rapport Mansions, Golders Green, and waited there all day?"

"That is so, m'sieu, but—"

"I haven't finished yet," said Rollison. "The man who old you to wait there and the man who told you to go to Charmion's place—was it the same man?"

"No, no, m'sieu! The first, 'e was a little man, so funnee in 'is face, with an absurd little nose—like—" she

135

paused, then hurried on: "a beak, m'sieu, the nose of a parrot!"

"Good!" said Rollison, with feeling. "The other?"

" 'E ees not so easy to describe," said Fifi, frowning; " 'E ees just a man, m'sieu, 'e—" she paused, then raised her hands helplessly. "Just a man!"

"Wearing dark clothes, a bowler hat, and carrying an umbrella," said Rollison, "pale-faced, ordinary-looking, and with his lips—" he pursed his lips a little, giving himself an odd, complacent expression—"like this?"

"M'sieu!" cried Fifi. "You know 'eem!"

"I'm beginning to think I do," admitted Rollison. "See if Grice is at the Yard, Jolly." He lit a cigarette after Fifi had refused one, and then gently he broke the news of Hilda's death. He did not tell her the circumstances, and was glad, for her distress surprised him. He knew that it would revive her anxiety for Joe, but she did not speak of that, just relapsed into silence and looked about the flat, as if helpless and hopeless.

"Mr. Grice is on the line, sir," said Jolly.

"Hallo, Grice," said Rollison. "How are things?"

Grice said, explosively: "If you've called me up to ask me 'how are things' I'll—"

"Oh, that was just a preliminary canter," the Toff assured him. "Seriously, have you anything in the way of results?"

"Nothing at all," said Grice, "except that I know you've been to Charmion's place and that his brother and sister-in-law were there. They slipped my man."

"They're at a little club in Littleton Place—remember it?" He did not wait for Grice to answer. "You should, for you told me about it—it's Grade 2 in your club system. Port Street, for the first grade, Littleton Place for the second grade, with its dancing, extravagance and what-have-you. They work there and call it a cabaret."

"The Charmions?" Grice sounded incredulous. "They're not under that name, I'll swear to that!"

"A Charmion by any other name smells just as foul," said Rollison. "The younger man and his wife did all

136

they could to make sure that I visited the club—to-night, I think, I'll be expected. I can't explain more now, but I thought you'd like to know."

"Will you be in if I come round right away?" asked Grice.

"No," said Rollison, emphatically. "I'm going to keep that date! I've done everything I've been asked to in this show so far, I don't see why I should stop now. But I'll amplify it a bit. The younger Charmions blame Guy, our parrot-like Guy, and also Charmion's wife, for her distressing habit of taking drugs. Charmion himself isn't sure whether they're telling the truth or not—at least, that's the attitude he adopts. He does it well, too; there are times when I think he's telling the truth and others when I think he's fooling me very nicely. However, that will work out. Concerning Golders Green—"

"Just a moment!" implored Grice. "Why?"

"A block of flats at Golders Green," insisted Rollison. "Bowler Hat went to one, didn't he? Could it have been Rapport Mansions?" When Grice did not immediately reply, he went on: "Don't say you've forgotten that Sergeant Wilson reported—"

"It was Rapport Mansions," said Grice, heavily.

"Bill, we are in the course of making the biggest fools of ourselves that we are ever likely to make."

"I wish to goodness you'd explain what you're talking about!"

"I can't—I don't know," said Rollison blandly, "except that I have a clear idea at the moment, and if I weren't the butt of the business I'd find it really funny. Still, it will be funny for someone before it's over. The thing is, old man—have Rapport Mansions watched, as well as your two clubs, will you? Keep your men at Mrs. Charmion's place and also at the lesser Charmion's. Make them large men, with very flat feet."

"But—" began Grice.

"Because," said Rollison earnestly, "we are being given all these addresses as places requiring attention. We are being directed with much skill to spend precious time

137

and on watching them—and who are we to refuse? We are invited to jump into a morass of impossibilities—well, let's jump. Shall we meet in the morning?"

"Rollison!" cried Grice.

"Let's say ten-thirty," said Rollison, and rang off.

He was not surprised to find Fifi looking at him as if he had taken leave of <u>his</u> senses, and Jolly regarding him with mild surprise. He beamed at them and lit another cigarette.

"Grice is cursing me," he said. "The ingratitude of policemen. Fifi, get to bed. Joe will be all right, they don't want to do any harm to him. Jolly, if anyone should call, I've gone to an Arabian Night's Entertainment, and I won't be back until morning." He buttoned his raincoat about him and stepped to the door, still high on the wave of optimism which had seized him when he had last spoken to Charmion, and which he believed would carry him through to the final phase.

Dark thoughts—the deaths of Hilda and Anderson being most insistent—kept entering his mind, but he repressed them firmly. His mission was for the living, not for the dead. He strolled through the rain towards Littleton Place, until he reached Number 1A. He was not surprised to find it a little difficult to enter; there were two closed doors and two peep-holes, and it cost him ten pound notes before he entered a little foyer, and, from somewhere above his head, heard the strains of hot rhythm. There was nothing about the club, the very name of which he did not know, which seemed in any way different from a hundred others which opened like mushrooms and were plucked away by the heavy hand of the law as soon as their law-breaking became too blatant.

Three doors led from the foyer.

One led, in turn, to a flight of steps carpeted with coconut-matting—the foyer was also covered with the same material—but the others were closed, or almost closed. He thought he saw a flurry of movement at one, which was ajar, and fancied that the handle of the other turned, very slightly.

A middle-aged, comely-looking woman took his hat, coat and gloves; she did not seem the type to be at a night-club, thought Rollison fleetingly. Armed with a card which declared him to be a club member, he went towards the stairs. He was quite sure that he was watched, equally sure that he had been right, and that the lesser Charmions had deliberately enticed him here. How much of their story was true did not greatly matter; he discounted most of it. All he knew was that they wanted him at this club, and that he was here to oblige them.

A gust of laughter and a blast of saxophone music, both equally raucous, came down the stairs as he sauntered up them. At the top of the stairs a little man, with a beak of a nose and tufts of grey hair over his eyes, regarded him expressionlessly and said:

"Good evening, sir."

Rollison congratulated himself on keeping an impassive face; for this man was Guy—he had been described so often that there could be no mistake.

And yet—

"Good evening," said the Toff, heavily. The beak of a nose fascinated him.

"Are you alone, sir?"

"Unhappily, yes," said the Toff.

"I think, perhaps," said the little man, "that you will find some amusing companions here."

"Good!" said Rollison.

He did not think that the little man was referring to ladies of leisure; there was something else in the man's voice, not menace, but a veiled amusement, perhaps even mockery. Expecting nothing except surprise, Rollison stepped through into the room, which was larger than he had expected.

On the dance floor in the centre—just in front of a dais on which a coloured orchestra played with wild abandon

—were eight or nine men, all small, like a troupe of gaily-clad acrobats. Scattered about were the club's patrons, nearly all young.

The troupe on the dance floor held the audience enraptured—and also fascinated the Toff, for each of them had a little, parrot-like nose, a receding chin and grey, bushy eyebrows.

CHAPTER XVII

VASTLY AMUSING

The little door-keeper was at Rollison's side, ostensibly guiding him towards a vacant table. Rollison looked down on him.

"Vastly amusing," he remarked.

"I thought you would find it so," said the little man. "I will send a waiter to you, sir."

"Thank you," said Rollison. "Can I get a drink?"

"With supper, sir, yes." The man's voice did not alter in tone, but the hint of mockery remained; his eyes were expressionless, but seemed to mock at the Toff, who sat down slowly and looked at the antics of the men on the dance-floor. They were acrobats of great skill, and, of course, each man wore a mask—a mask exactly like that of the effigy.

Much was made depressingly clear.

He had thought that by finding the manufacturer of the mask and the others he would trace the little man named Guy, and here were eight—nine—*ten* of them, including the door-keeper, for each of whom a mask had been made. It meant that his one real clue faded into thin air, and he was left holding the stuffed canvas of the effigy.

The little men, all clad in riotous colours, were flinging themselves about the dance-floor, on each other's backs, under each other's legs, sprawling here and jumping there, bounding up and thudding down, to the throbbing rhythm of the Negro band and little squeaks of delight from the actors; laughter, high-pitched and almost hysterical, came from the people at the tables.

There were at least a hundred couples.

A waiter approached Rollison, and he looked up—and stared, again trying hard not to reveal his feelings.

"Good evening, sir," said the waiter, calmly, placing a menu card in front of him. "I am afraid it is too late for dinner, but everything else is available."

"Ah, thanks," said Rollison.

He looked away from the man, yet could see him clearly in his mind's eye. Dressed in formal waiter's clothes, tails and white tie and boiled shirt, the waiter's expression was impassive; his lips were pushed forward slightly, as if he were about to whistle, and it gave him an air of half-amused complacency—at just such an expression in the Toff, Fifi had been astonished. In short, it was the man of the bowler hat and the furled umbrella.

"I will have some lemonade," said Rollison.

He wanted to see the man's face drop, but was disappointed; there was no change in that smug expression. Rollison half-regretted his 'lemonade,' but he wanted to send some message to whoever had arranged this farcical reception, to let them know that he saw the joke. Then, looking away from the dancing men—whose turns grew fiercer and faster and whose squeaks of delight were outdone only by the unnatural laughter of the revellers—he saw other waiters.

They were not exactly like the man who had served him, but had he seen any one of them, he would have imagined that he had found the bowler-hatted man who had haunted him.

The waiter returned; Rollison put a pound note on the tray as the lemonade, complete with straw, was placed in front of him. He was given twelve shillings and sixpence change. He left a half-crown on the tray, and said:

"How long do you stay open?"

"Indefinitely, sir, for soft drinks," said the waiter, and went off, leaving Rollison with a distinct impression that his joke had rebounded. He sipped the lemonade, charily; and then he looked at it again, trying not to start; it was a whisky and soda, fairly strong, with a peculiar tang to it—something he could not identify.

The room was tawdrily furnished and decorated. Once there had been an effort to brighten it, and there were daubs of silver paint on the walls, and faint outlines of grotesque, nude figures; the ceiling had been distempered, and the distemper was flaking in a dozen places. The dais was covered with red plush, the only new-looking piece in the room. But the napery was spotless and the silver sparkled.

Then he saw two people who put all thought of the little men and the waiters out of his mind.

They were sitting at a table near the front, the man unsmiling, the woman with him—sleek, dark-haired, a languorous beauty with great, dark eyes—was smiling with detached amusement; he was not altogether sure of the woman's identity, but he surmised that it was Blanding's wife.

The man was certainly Sir Roland Blanding.

Rollison stared, and then said, gently:

"Ye-es, vastly amusing. I wonder how Georgina is?"

He looked about him for other familiar faces, and hardly knew whether to be pleased or sorry at seeing them. Only the Blandings were there, watching without great interest.

The band was working itself up to a pitch of frenzy; there was little resemblance to music, only a rhythm which seemed to touch the depths of ancient African voodoo. The little men had worked themselves up to a fine pitch, their posturing and gestures obscene; and yet, Rollison knew, they did not step outside the law. Faster and faster they went, until it seemed as if they must drop from sheer exhaustion; and then with a crash the music stopped. The little men began to run from the dance floor, not towards the rear of the room but towards the door through which Rollison had entered. They did not pause until they reached his table; then each one pirouetted and raised his head in a mockery so refined and telling that Rollison had to smile. Each one in turn revolved in front of him, arms akimbo, head held high, and then ran on towards the door, held open by the tenth man.

As the last went by, Rollison mused:

"And *one* of them is Guy."

A ripple of laughter from the rest of the crowd made him look back towards the dance floor; he recognized Charmion's brother, who began a silly dance, a piece of buffoonery that was genuinely funny; his wife joined him, clad in a skirt of feathers and a brassière to match; she looked quite beautiful. Charmion was dressed in old clothes, cloth cap and choker, to contrast with the smooth pallor of her flesh; and they began a dance certainly not inspired in England. It suited the temper of the crowd to perfection, but in the middle of it Blanding rose from his table.

His wife said something; Blanding's answer travelled even as far as Rollison's ears.

"No," he said. "We're going."

A few people looked at his tall, distinguished figure, but most of the revellers were intent only upon the Charmions. Blanding placed his wife's cloak about her close-fitting gold-trimmed black gown, and then led the way to the door. Rollison waited until he was a couple of yards away, then stood up, smiling. Blanding saw him for the first time, and started.

"Good evening," he said.

"Hallo," smiled Rollison. "Our night out, isn't it?" Lady Blanding eyed him with a smile of vague amusement; she was, thought, Rollison, a queen amongst the rabble at the club.

Blanding presented him, with more haste than courtesy.

"What are you doing at this place, Rollison?"

"On a quest," murmured Rollison. "A quest for adventure and excitement. Aren't we all? Won't you sit down?" He waited, and Blanding hesitated; the waiter came up. "Do stay," he said. "It's not so appalling from here."

"Appalling?" echoed Blanding.

"So it isn't what you like?" murmured Lady Blanding;

144

there was no doubt that she looked at Rollison with admiration. "Let us stay for a few minutes longer, Roland."

"Oh, yes—yes m'dear," said Blanding. He seemed put out, conscious of it, and annoyed by it. "I didn't expect to find—what *are* you doing here, Rollison? You can speak freely, my wife knows all about what has happened."

"I shan't know what I want here until I've had time to ponder over it," said Rollison. "How's 'Gina?" He looked delighted when Blanding told him that, according to Dr. Race, Georgina would be perfectly all right with treatment provided she was handled with understanding and sympathy for the next few weeks.

"But for you, Mr. Rollison, we might not have suspected the trouble," said Lady Blanding.

"Oh, I don't know," said Rollison deprecatingly. "These things get out. Er—Charmion, now. You recognized him, of course."

"I did. I think he recognized me," said Blanding.

"He wouldn't be slow at that," said the Toff. "So it is the same man? And Georgina, of course, knew of the bother you'd had with a Charmion and was therefore surprised when she read the name this mornig. That was enough to upset her, together with the bad news from Teddy Marchant. Nothing else?"

"I don't think so," said Blanding.

"That's fine!" said Rollison, and smiled tentatively. "I'd like to ask what you're doing here. Dare I?"

"Georgina is a member of this club," said Blanding, with such an attitude and expression of disgust that Rollison had to hide a smile. "She told us that, and I thought I might do some good by coming."

"Ah! Because you thought she bought the drug here," mused Rollison. "The obvious is always the right explanation, isn't it? Oh, I'm sorry—" the waiter, standing impassively by them, coughed slightly. "What will you have? The lemonade is good," he added, "and they might have—"

145

"Nothing, thanks," said Blanding hastily. "We must go." He pushed his chair back. His wife rose, but she seemed reluctant.

"Must you?" asked the Toff, regretfully. "Blanding, may I advise you once again? Mud sticks. This place is mud from floor to ceiling, door to window. Very nasty, smelly, oleaginous, which you might not be able to deal with by ordinary cleansing methods." He smiled, a little inanely, expecting an annoyed frown on Blanding's face. But Blanding made no comment, only his wife smiled—that vague yet unmistakable smile, as if she were amused and wanted to tell Rollison why, but could not quite summon the energy. "Well, if you must go," Rollison said, "Good night. My love to 'Gina."

Lady Blanding offered her hand; her pressure was firm. Blanding bowed, and they went out, with the first man who might have been called Guy bowing low before them.

The music reached a faster tempo, the Charmions were keeping the audience on tenterhooks of excitement; and that excitement, which had its unnatural element and was at all times unpleasant, told the Toff that most of them were either drunk or drug-ridden. But as he looked about him he knew that it would be almost impossible to prove it.

That was not all.

If Grice came here, he would recognize the man at the door as the man whom the girl at Marlborough Street had described as the one who had sold her cocaine; but he could not arrest all nine. If Fifi were to identify the man who had sent her to Charmion, and who thus confessed his knowledge of the whereabouts of Joe, she would be confounded by the appearance of the others. Deliberately the Toff had been led here, deliberately given reason to suppose that he would get results—and then it had all been thrown into his face, a grandiose hoax.

The Charmions had lured him here; but, even if he

brought that home to them, would it help him to find who had prompted them?

Above all, what was the motive?

A man approached him as the Charmions finished their turn; the man was small, well-dressed, inconspicuous and yet, somehow, impressive. He spoke to several other people and then neared Rollison's table.

"Is everything quite satisfactory, sir?"

"Why, yes," said Rollison with gusto. "Everything's fine! Just"—he beamed—"as I expected."

He thought the man looked startled.

"I'm very glad to hear that, sir. Who recommended you to come? You will forgive me if the question appears to be impertinent, but—"

"Impertinent?" asked Rollison, astonished. "Certainly not! The thing is, I don't know who recommended me—shall we say I had a number of hints?" He smiled more widely and went on in a soft, caressing voice: "You are, I suppose, the manager?"

"Yes, and at your service."

"Good," said Rollison. "Splendid! Give the proprietor a message for me, will you?"

"I will give a message to the Club Committee," said the manager, promptly.

"A committee, is there?" mused Rollison. "Better still, they'll know all about it. Tell them that I received the hints, that I admire the scenery, but—" his smile was positively effusive "—the play is poor. Very poor. It wants new lines, it's old and stilted."

"I don't quite understand—" began the manager, but his expression was set; he was alarmed.

"Oh, no, you wouldn't," said Rollison. "After all, you only do what you're told. But they will. Tell them that I've seen it so often that I'm more than a little tired of it, and that if they'd really wanted it to succeed they should have—" he paused.

"Yes, sir?" said the manager, politely, but still looking apprehensive.

"They should have made a clean sweep," said Rollison. "The trouble is that there are too many of the old cast in the play. Especially the curtain-raiser."

"Curtain-raiser, sir?"

"Yes, of course," said the Toff. "That's all we've seen so far, isn't it? But the stage is set for the real piece, I think." He beamed. "Am I bewildering you? Never mind, tell the committee just what I say, and tell them—" he paused again, still smiling, although with a different expression in his eyes.

"Yes, sir?" said the manager.

"Tell them that they shouldn't have killed Hilda and Anderson," said Rollison.

"I assure you, sir, that I do not—"

"Understand?" said the Toff, softly. "Perhaps you don't, but they will. Tell them I've a few new lines which should put some pep into the show before the end of the last act. Tell them—" he rested a hand on the other's shoulder and pressed hard—"tell them that they will be free for about another forty-eight hours—if they're lucky. Is that clear? Forty-eight hours. I think that's all." He stood up, and, doing so, upset the glass of 'lemonade'; it spread quickly about the white cloth, and began to drip on to the floor. "They'll topple over just like that," said Rollison, "because I *know*, my friend. Anderson told me; he did not die as quickly as they wished. Have you got it straight?"

"I think you must be drunk," said the manager. "Perhaps you would like to see the members of the Club Committee and lodge your complaint with them in person?"

"Complaint?" echoed the Toff. "What Complaint? This is a declaration of faith! Good night!"

He strode off, leaving the man standing and staring after him. He reached the door and hurried down, ignoring the door-keeper. The buxom, pleasant woman in charge of the cloak-room fetched his coat and hat and wished him a pleasant good-night; he left her half a crown and went out into the damp night air, not quite sure whether he had made a fool of himself or not.

He passed two shadowy figures not far from the front door, and, suddenly, turned on his heel and approached one.

"Are you from Scotland Yard?" he asked. "I'm Rollison."

"Oh—yes, yes, sir, that's right." The man, whose face was just a pale blur in the darkness, drew nearer and dropped his voice to a conspiratorial whisper. "Anything doing in there to-night?"

"Plenty," said Rollison, "but not quite enough to take action, although that'll come. Good night."

"Good night, sir."

The voice echoed after him—and the word. 'Good night,' from Lady Blanding and Blanding himself, the manager, the waiter, the door-keeper, the woman at the cloakroom. 'Good night, good night!' It followed him like a will-o'-the-wisp, a fugitive thing which might be simply formal but might be filled with meaning. '*Good night!*'

He stopped when he reached Gresham Terrace and took himself to task.

"It just won't do," he said aloud. "They're doing what they want to, they've got me on the raw and guessing."

He went to his flat, knowing that he had admitted the truth; his one vague hope was that his exuberant bluff with the manager might make his adversaries start guessing too.

CHAPTER XVIII

"GOOD MORNING"

"Good morning, sir," said Jolly.

The Toff opened his eyes and peered about his room; Jolly was pulling the curtains apart, and a tray was by the side of the bed, with the papers and the post. The Toff hitched himself up on his pillows and looked at his man. Then he remembered the fantastic interlude at the club at Littleton Place, and that when he had reached the flat he had gone straight to bed, saying little even to Jolly. He had waited just long enough to inquire about Fifi, and to be told that she was in the spare room, fast asleep.

"Good morning," he said. "Pour out for me, Jolly."

"Very good, sir." The manservant stood for a moment in a shaft of sunlight, which made Rollison frown; the sun was not usually up when he was called. "It is nearly half-past eight, sir," said Jolly, "I thought I had better let you sleep a little longer, since you were in so late last night."

"Yes," smiled Rollison. "Thanks. Ten little indians—no, little parrot-men, Jolly. Ten! And men with umbrellas—five or six; there might have been more, I didn't see them all. Jolly, we're stymied."

"I can't believe that you will not be able to get out of it."

"I can," said Rollison. "I can see complete failure. Because the truth of this is beyond me, Jolly!" He sipped his tea and gave his man a detailed description of what had happened at the club, including everything he remembered saying, and then: "When I was in the cold night air, Jolly, I knew that I had been talking for the sake of it, just empty vapouring; I doubt whether that smooth-faced little customer did more than grin behind my back. He and his committee!"

"There *is* a committee at the club, sir," said Jolly, mildly. "Incidentally, it is called—"

"Go on," said Rollison, his expression growing strained.

"The Parrot Club, sir."

"Oh, my sainted aunt!" exclaimed the Toff. "It can't be! All right, all right, if you say so—how did you learn all this?"

"My friend Mr. Lauriston telephoned a short while ago," said Jolly. "The mask was one of a dozen made by *Romain Frères* of Paris—they have their studios in this country now, sir—and the eyes were made by a small firm in the Midlands—a one-man business, I understand. Eyes were made for each mask, sir."

"Oh," said Rollison.

"The masks were supplied to the Parrot Club by *Romain Frères* some six months ago, sir," Jolly told him, "and I asked whether anything was known of the club. It is primarily a dancing club."

"Ah," murmured Rollison, and poured out another cup of tea.

"The committee, which buys from Lauriston and *Romain Frères* from time to time—they supply dresses, theatrical make-up, wigs, and the usual accessories, sir—is a most respectable one," said Jolly.

"Guinea-pigs," murmured Rollison.

"Probably, sir, but quite respectable. I expect Mr. Grice knows all about it."

"Yes. So we sink lower and lower into gloom, Jolly."

"There *must* be something behind it, sir."

"Oh, I shouldn't be surprised," said Rollison, "although if it weren't for the murders I'd begin to wonder whether it weren't a gigantic hoax to make me feel a fool —which is putting it mildly. There aren't murders without motives. How's Fifi?"

"She requested permission to prepare breakfast, sir," said Jolly.

"How does she seem? Still depressed?"

"I wouldn't say that, sir. She seems quite confident that the mystery will be solved. By assuring her that Link will be all right you have removed her greatest fear, of course." Jolly looked sombre. "Had you any grounds for thus reassuring her, sir?"

Rollison frowned. "No, no grounds. Only convictions. Only convictions." He shrugged. "One can but try."

It was not a successful morning.

Grice telephoned, instead of calling in person; the inquest on Hilda would be the following day, and that on Anderson would be a little later on the same day. Grice did not rub it in, but Rollison knew that the story of the finding of Hilda's body would have come out at the inquest, and the Press would be there in strength, since there was a connection with Anderson's murder. Certainly they would be at Anderson's inquest in batallions. For once he had omitted to look at the papers in bed, and, at breakfast—just after Grice had telephoned—he looked through them. All, including the sober *Gazette*, linked his name with that of Hilda Brent's death as well as Anderson's. There was nothing unpleasant, no hint that the Press knew the full story, but the *Gazette*'s telltale words: '*It is understood that Scotland Yard have questioned the Hon. Richard Rollison in connection with both murders*', would certainly be round London in a matter of hours. He knew that if he showed his face in the West End he would be importuned from all sides.

Fifi grew more anxious.

Young Bob Moor telephoned, soon after ten o'clock, to ask whether Rollison needed him for anything, and Rollison side-tracked the youngster. Grice came at last, listened to the full story, and was mildly disapproving; in truth, he was also disappointed. The reports of the men whom he had placed to watch the homes of the greater and lesser Charmions offered nothing, like those of the men who had watched the flats at Golders Green and the Parrot Club—whose committee was a stumbling-block of the first order, for it included the most reputable citizens.

Grice agreed that behind those names the real directors of the club moved.

"What can I do about it?" Grice demanded. "I've raided it twice. No drugs, no broken rules—"

"They served me with a whisky and soda last night," Rollison said coldly. "Can't you get them to do the same to a plain-clothes man? I mean, even that would be a charge of some kind."

"Don't fool," chided Grice.

"I'm left with nothing else to do," said Rollison. "Whom haven't I seen? Mrs. Charmion—the dope-raddled wife."

"I've seen her," said Grice.

"No good?"

"Nearly certifiable, and almost bedridden," said Grice. "Certainly no good. I'm told that she gets very violent."

"But Anderson found something; he had no more to go on than we have," Rollison pointed out. "Hilda Brent knew something—"

"Yes, I know," said Grice, "but I'm no farther on than you are. What I am going to do is to question every one of the waiters and the parrot-dancers at the club, but I don't think I shall get anything from them."

Grice went off to report to the Assistant Commissioner and to interview the dancers and waiters; he telephoned in the middle of the afternoon to say that he had obtained nothing of consequence from any of them, and that it was impossible for him to make any kind of charge. The girl who had been at Marlborough Street had identified four of the little men in succession, so her evidence was useless.

Fifi was rapidly becoming tearful; she could not understand why 'M'sieu Roll'son' stayed at the flat and did not go out to find her Joe. Nor could she understand the change in Charmion—she did not believe, she said, that it was Charmion.

"But he is," insisted Rollison. "He went to prison and came out. You don't change your identity in prison," he added, and Fifi went into voluble protestations that she was quite sure that no man could change so much. Finally:

"I do not believe eet! 'E ees not Charmion! The othair —pairhaps, but not the one you talk to, m'sieu! Where are your eyes?" She screwed up her own and pointed a stubby forefinger at one. "Where are they, m'sieu? *Hein!* There was a time when all of you was eyes, now—why do you not look, m'sieu?"

Rollison, feeling that he deserved this, did not resent it.

He found himself thinking about the Blandings. He had been inclined to take the man's story of his presence at the Parrot Club at its face value, but now he began to question it, although he admitted that it was because there was nothing else left to question. Then he thought, more soberly, of Georgina. By testing everything that had happened, turning it over in his mind a dozen times, he hoped to see a new facet. Of all the things that had happened, the queerest was the way Georgina had acted after she had seen that card and 'Charmion' in green ink. Since she was taking drugs, even a slight shock would affect her badly, because of her taut nerves; but Blanding had accounted for it because of Teddy Marchant's accident.

"It could be a little of both," said Rollison. He stretched out for the telephone and dialled Blanding's number. A maid answered him, and said:

"Sir Roland is not here, sir. I'm sorry."

"Is Lady Blanding there?"

"I'll find out, sir. Who is that, please?"

"Richard Rollison," said Rollison, and waited, not expecting Lady Blanding to speak to him and yet remembering the pressure of her hand when she had left him at the Parrot Club. Then her voice, languorous like her manner and her eyes, sounded over the telephone.

"Good afternoon, Mr. Rollison."

"Oh, good afternoon!" Rollison stirred himself, "I'm worried about Georgina, Lady Blanding. How is she?"

"She is still a little subdued," said Georgina's mother, puzzling him by her choice of word, "but I feel sure that

154

she will recover quite soon, and our gratitude to you will know no bounds."

'Know no bounds,' Rollison thought, and wondered testily whether the whole family talked in clichés; his impression of Blanding was of a man of ability but little imagination, a worthy fellow with few human vices and as little human understanding. Yet the man had behaved well, presumably, over Georgina; equally well over his own daughter. Aloud, he said: "I'm really glad to hear it."

"I suppose the truth is that you hoped to come to see her," said Mrs. Blanding.

"I had thought of it," said Rollison.

"Do come," said Lady Blanding, "she will be glad to see you, I feel sure. And she has told me about the strange little man who gave her the post card, Colonel Rollison. So bewildering, isn't it? I was telling her, you see, of the strange little men at the club, and how I disliked them, and she—"

She went on talking; Rollison did not hear a word. Like a sudden, blinding flash, a question hurled itself against his mind and dazzled him. He did not answer, even when Lady Blanding said, for the second time: "Don't you think so?"

"Oh, yes," said Rollison, hastily. "Yes, of course. Er—may I come right away?"

There was a pause, then a faint laugh.

"I don't think you are giving me your undivided attention," said Lady Blanding in gentle reproof. "That was what I had just said—that it would be better if you came at once. I shall look forward to seeing you."

Lady Blanding rang off, and Rollison looked a little stupidly at the receiver, then replaced it and stared at Jolly, who had tapped and entered. But Jolly did not speak; he noted the intensity of Rollison's gaze, and he stood quietly by the door after closing it softly. Rollison stared at the wall opposite, but showed that he was aware of his man's entrance, for he began to speak in a low-pitched voice:

"Something's slipped into place, Jolly. Georgina Scott was a member of the Parrot Club, yet her mother described the little men to her and apparently their description surprised her. The club bought the masks some time ago, so they're not new turns. Why doesn't Georgina, as a member of the club, recognize the little man at once?"

"The man who slipped her the post card?" asked Jolly. "I don't know, sir. It would seem reasonable that?"

"She'd recognize him at once, of course! And she did!" Rollison pushed his chair back and it banged against the wall. "Of course, she recognized him; that's what upset her, why she's cracked up. Not just because she recognized him as one of the little troupers, but because the man associated himself with Charmion." He looked excited. "Do you follow me?"

"I do, sir."

"And Georgina was the first to warn me what was happening," said Rollison. "She told me that it was because Teddy Marchant insisted; she made me think that she was gossiping for the sake of it. I even called her woolly-minded! Jolly, she deliberately lured me into the case. D'you get that? She did her damnedest to get me interested. Operative question—why?"

"You think she is involved, sir?" asked Jolly, faintly sceptical.

"She knew something—she must still know. She was frightened, she knew of me, she decided that a casual word would secure my interest—damn it, she even broke off at the crucial moment to make sure that I would be intrigued. Jolly, I hope to God I'm not too late."

"For—for Miss Georgina's safety, sir?" asked Jolly.

"Yes, and more," said Rollison. "Telephone Lady Diana Forrest at Hertford, and find out whether she has received any more strange visitors lately, will you?" He went out, passing Fifi with a wave of the hand and a preoccupied smile which made the Frenchwoman run to Jolly to demand what had happened.

Rollison went into the street, scowled because no cab was in sight, and decided that he would get to Portman

Place more quickly by walking than searching for a taxi. He reached the Blandings' house in a little over ten minutes, slackening his pace only when he was within sight of it; he did not want to create the impression that he had been hurrying.

A bicycle stood against the curb opposite.

Rollison noticed it vaguely. He rang the bell and knocked at the same time, being rewarded by a quick response; a maid, very much more alert and presentable than the girl who had been on duty the previous night, opened the door.

"Good afternoon," said Rollison, depositing his hat and gloves on the hall-stand. "Mr. Richard Rollison—Miss Georgina is expecting me. Is she in her room?"

"Yes, sir, but—"

Rollison left her standing and climbed the stairs. He reached Georgina's room, tapped briefly, and opened the door at once.

"Who's there?" cried Georgina.

Rollison forced a smile as he put his head round the door. Georgina was sitting up in bed and staring at him. She had on some flimsy wrap, and her hair was fluffy, her cheeks and lips were not made-up, but she had a natural charm which he thought an improvement on the sophisticated Georgina of his acquaintance. Her lips parted, and then she said:

"Do you always behave like this?"

"Oh, no," said Rollison, grandly; "only now and again, when I'm dealing with my favourite clients. How are you, 'Gina? If you're as good as you look you're an angelic example to us all." He advanced and held out his hand; hers was cool and her grip firm.

"I'm sorry I was such an absolute *heel*, last night," she said. "I just couldn't help it, it was one thing after the other."

"It's all right," said the Toff. " 'Gina, I want you to answer one question. That little man who pushed the card in your coat—you knew that he came from the Parrot Club, didn't you?"

Georgina stared at him; what little colour there had been in her lips faded. The brilliance of her eyes, almost a feverish brilliance, took on an expression which he had seen before—it was closely akin to terror.

"No, I didn't!" she denied. "I don't know why you should think I did; I'd never seen him before!" That she was lying was so transparent that for a moment Rollison was nonplussed. He stepped nearer, gripping her hands more tightly.

" 'Gina, listen to me. You called me on the telephone and warned me about this, you made sure of my interest, and you did it deliberately. For some reason you didn't want me to think you had done so, and for the same reason you wanted to make sure that your part in calling me in wasn't known, but—it's gone too far for personal loyalties. You're shielding someone, and you must stop. Two people have died, and others will die unless I know the whole truth—and you can help me to find it. 'Gina, I'm desperately serious." He paused, and then repeated: "*Desperately* serious. I tell you, two people have died."

She licked her lips.

"I—I'd never seen him before," she repeated, "except —except at the—at the Parrot Club. I thought he—he was one of the turns, they have a cabaret sometimes. That— that's all."

"There's more in it than that. If that were all you would have told me right away. If that were all you wouldn't have been so secretive about telling me that you were afraid. You *are* afraid, 'Gina."

She said, in a hushed voice:

"Yes. Yes, I'm terribly afraid!" Her cheeks were ashen and her eyes a burnished blue. "I'm terribly afraid," she whispered. "But I've told you—all—I dare."

"You must dare more!" said Rollison urgently. "Not for yourself—forget yourself, 'Gina, there are the others, perhaps many others."

"Please!" she said. "I can't tell you, I daren't tell you. I —I won't tell you, because it might not be true!"

She leaned back on the pillows, with her eyes closed

and the dark, beautiful lashes fringing them; beneath her eyes were shadows, dark and tell-tale, but he did not think it was because of the drugs that he had imagined her to be taking, he did not think there was any other reason than fear, a deep-rooted, paralyzing fear which had made her turn to him.

He released her hands and looked about the room. In one corner, near the other side of the bed, was a white telephone. He moved round the bed and picked up the receiver, wondering why he had been allowed to stay in the room so long. He dialled Scotland Yard and asked for Grice, praying that the man would be there; he was, and he sounded gruff.

"Yes, Rolly, what is it?"

"Will you send a police-surgeon or any doctor you can really trust to the Blandings' place—27, Portman Square —and then watch for a Dr.—". He tried to recall the name of the doctor Blanding had called the previous night; it was a short one, rhyming with 'lace'. "Race," he said. "Dr. Race, somewhere in the West End. Don't let him go; have every move he makes watched—you'll do this, Grice?"

After a brief pause, Grice said: "All right."

"Good man!" said Rollison, with feeling. "One other thing—Charmion's wife. Have her protected, have the flats carefully watched. If you can, get her history." He added, after a moment's deliberation: "I think we're nearly there."

Then he replaced the receiver, turned—and found a little man with a face like a parrot, who might have been any one of the troupers he had seen the night before, standing in front of the satinwood wardrobe against the wall opposite. The little man held a small automatic almost negligently; but there was nothing casual in his expression; his beady eyes were malignant and inflamed with rage.

"So you think you're nearly there, do you?" he said. "Think again, Rollison. *Pick up that receiver and cancel your instructions to Grice.*"

CHAPTER XIX

MORE OF THE MAN
NAMED GUY

"Oh, hallo," said the Toff, dry-lipped. "Mr. Guy, I presume?"

"Don't try to be funny," said the little man. His lips barely moved, the words were audible because of the hush in the room. "Pick up that receiver and cancel your instructions to Grice."

"In the first place," said Rollison, without moving, "I don't instruct the police to do anything, I request. In the second, once—"

"Pick up—" began Guy, only to stop as the Toff cut across his words regretfully, putting everything he could into a pretence at being unconcerned.

"I just can't do it, Guy. The wheels of the law grind slowly, but they grind. Oh, yes, they grind. Grice will come himself, I think."

"Unless you pick up the receiver and do as I have told you, you will see Georgina Scott killed in front of your eyes," said Guy. "I am not joking. You have time to prevent it. You can tell Grice it was a mistake. I don't care how you do it, but do it. I shall count three, do you understand?" It might have been the wax model speaking, so little did the lips move, so hushed was the voice. "One," he added. "I'm serious."

Rollison snapped: "Don't be a—"

"Two," said Guy. He raised his gun, training it on Georgina, who appeared to be unconscious and whose breast was moving very gently beneath her wrap.

"Don't do it!" snapped Rollison. He picked up the telephone and dialled the Yard number—the eyes of the little man were on him. Had he dialled any number but Whitehall 1212 the shot would have been fired. Yet Guy looked at Rollison, his narrowed eyes still holding the malignance which puzzled Rollison. "Scotland Yard?" Rollison asked. "Superintendent Grice, please—an urgent call from Richard Rollison."

"Don't try to convey a hidden message," said Guy.

Rollison said, slowly:

"I can guarantee nothing, but . . . hallo, Grice?"

"I'm sorry, sir," said a respectful voice, "but the Superintendent has just left the office. I'll try to find out where he is, if you'll hold on."

"Oh," said Rollison. "Yes, I'll hold on." He looked at the other and said, much more casually than he felt: "Grice isn't in his office."

"Countermand his orders to his staff," said Guy.

"Oddly enough, they don't accept my orders," said Rollison. He felt a pulse beating in his neck, and a film of sweat on his forehead. If the man would shift the gun an inch, if Georgina would move her position—he had a wild thought of putting his hands beneath the bed and heaving it over on one side, so that Georgina would be hidden; he would have tried, but there was not sufficient time. He wanted anything to happen to relieve the tension which smothered the temporary exultation he had felt when the man had first spoken; for that order had not been a hoax, it had been grimly serious. It meant that he had asked Grice to do something of which this man was afraid.

Well, Grice would do it. Whatever happened to Georgina and himself, Grice would act.

The doctor, of course—Dr. Race. A man he had never seen, a man of whom he had heard only once. But there were others, many others; Rollison thought that he saw half of it, although there was much which would have to unfold itself.

"Rollison, if—" the man began.

Rollison said: "There's nothing more that I can do." He thought it might be worth trying to throw the telephone at the man; it would at least make him jump and spoil his aim. "Nothing you can do will save you. If you do more murder—"

He placed his leg against the side of the bed; it was useless to try to overturn it, but he could shift it to one side. He exerted all the pressure he could, and the bed groaned, then moved a couple of inches. The man named Guy fired. A bullet cut through Georgina's hair and pillow, and buried itself in the wood or the wall behind; there was little sound, for the automatic had a silencer. He pushed again as Guy swung the gun round towards him.

Georgina, suddenly awake, screamed!

Rollison darted towards the wall.

The bullet from Guy's gun caught him in the fleshy part of the left forearm; he felt the stinging pain of the wound and the numbness which seized his arm at the moment of the impact. He struck against the wall, without taking his eyes off Guy, and shouted at the top of his voice to attract attention; and Georgina screamed again.

Rollison knew that he could not evade the inevitable second bullet from Guy—but with his right hand he snatched up the telephone and as he moved it in front of him the bullet struck it; the instrument disintegrated in his hand, he felt a sharp stinging sensation, but nothing else; the bullet ricochetted into the wall.

In the passage someone called out in alarm, and there were hurried footsteps. Below, in the street, the engine of a car started up and a car moved off. Had Guy fired again he must have wounded Rollison grievously, but the man turned and moved swiftly to the window, not looking away but for a moment unable to train his gun accurately. The man was so desperately anxious to find out what car was moving that he took a chance which enabled Rollison to put his right hand into his pocket and clutch his own atutomatic. He fired through his pocket in the hope of wounding Guy, but the bullet struck the man in the head; he had not allowed for his small stature.

Guy dropped his gun and stood quite still. On his face was an expression of consternation and surprise; it remained there as his knees bent and he fell down—just as the footsteps reached the door and someone began to hammer on it.

Only then did Rollison realize that the door was locked.

He judged that Guy had entered while he had been absorbed in questioning Georgina. He stepped swiftly across the room, holding his left hand against his side; two drops of blood fell from it and were bright on the creamy carpet. Rollison opened the door with his left hand so that he could keep the doorway covered with his gun; then he stepped aside, for it was Blanding and young Moor.

"Rol—" began Blanding, and then saw the automatic. He drew back a pace as Moor cried:

"'*Gina!*'" and rushed past Rollison towards the girl, who had hitched herself up on her pillow and was staring, terror-stricken, towards the huddled body of Guy.

"The police should be here in ten minutes," said Rollison in a low-pitched voice. "'Gina's not hurt."

"She'll need a doctor," Blanding said, agitatedly. "Rollison, what on earth have you been doing? Look at—" he stared at Guy, and broke off.

"A doctor, yes," said Rollison, "'Phone your man. This telephone's no good, find another." He felt the blood pouring from the wound in his arm, and began to take off his coat. "Hurry, man!" The doctor was not likely to come, of course, although there was just a chance that he would not know what had happened, that he had been betrayed; first by accident and then by Guy's manner. "Oh, Blanding! Did someone leave in a car just now?"

Blanding called over his shoulder as he hurried down a passage:

"My wife went—"

"Come back!" cried Rollison, his coat half off. "Your wife went where? Tell me, man, where did she go?"

"I think she's gone out to a bridge party," said Blanding, without stopping.

163

Rollison turned back, passed Georgina's room and went into another, opposite; it was a bathroom, as he had seen through the doorway. He finished taking off his coat and picked up a hand towel. Taking a pair of scissors from the bathroom cabinet he nicked the hem, then ripped the towel so that he had a two-inch strip. He tied it above the ugly wound in his arm, watching the blood well up. He used a propelling pencil as a tourniquet and the bleeding slackened. He made as neat a job as he could of bathing the wound, although it still bled a little, then wrapped the rest of the towel about it.

When he reached the passage again, Blanding was going into Georgina's room.

Bob Moor was standing looking down at her, wide-eyed and helpless. Georgina was saying:

"Go away, go away, go away!"

Rollison reached Moor and took his shoulder; he motioned towards the door. Moor's frightened, worried eyes were turned towards him reproachfully, but the youngster obeyed. Blanding began to question Georgina, but she shrieked at him to go. She was panting with emotion. "Go away, go away!" she cried, "I can't stand any more, I can't stand it!"

"But my dear," said Blanding, helplessly. "I only want to help you."

"Go away!" shrieked Georgina.

"You've got to help her!" cried Moor, from the door; he had gone no farther than the passage and was in the room again hurrying towards her. "You've got to give her something to quieten her, can't you see she'll go mad? Oh, 'Gina, 'Gina!" He reached her side, pushing past the Toff and shouldering Blanding out of the way. "Darling, tell me—" he put a hand to her face, as if to try to close her mouth, which was wide open as she screamed. Rollison saw a little white thing, like a pill, against her tongue; it seemed to appear from nowhere. "Darling, don't scream like that, don't—" went on Moor, as if distracted.

164

Rollison took two long strides and reached him; he swung his clenched right fist, catching the youth under the jaw. All the power he could summon was in the blow, which sent Moor flying against the wall, his eyes rolling. Blanding stared stupidly, Georgina began to quieten down, gasping instead of shrieking; her mouth was closed.

"Get her mouth open," Rollison said, savagely, "Pinch her nose—get her mouth open. Go on!" His voice was so harsh that Blanding obeyed, like a man in a dream, jerking Georgina's head as if preparing to administer medicine to a recalcitrant child. Rollison stood over her, inserting his little finger into her mouth; Blanding let go, and Georgina's teeth bit into the finger, but Rollison kept it there; he felt the tablet. "Get her mouth open!" he repeated, and as it opened he hooked the tablet out; it dropped to the sheet. "All right," he said, and turned to little Robert Moor, who was picking himself up and who had his right hand at his hip pocket.

"Keep away," he said. He had stopped pretending; his eyes were cold and dangerous as the Toff approached him. "Keep away!" He snatched out a gun, but the Toff was too close and hooked his legs from under him; he fell, dropping the gun. "We're making progress," the Toff said, but his head was reeling and he felt faint. Georgina's face seemed to be describing ever-widening circles, Blanding was bobbing up and down. He was vaguely aware of surprise at the discovery of the treachery of the innocent-seeming Robert Moor. As he staggered to the bed and sat down, putting his face in his hands, he muttered something—he wanted to make sure that Blanding did not allow Moor to get at his gun. The words would not form themselves properly. A great blackness came over him, and he knew that he was on the point of fainting. He put his head between his knees, grunting with the effort. He grew aware of confused sounds and fresh voices, a hand on his shoulder and a question which became more and more urgent.

"Rollison, are you all right?"

He straightened up; a moving face in front of him was familiar and friendly. It was Grice.

"Moor," he mouthed. "Man named Moor. Get him."

"He won't do any harm," Grice said.

Someone was bending over Georgina, who was now lying quite still. Blanding loomed large over Rollison and Grice told him, sharply, to get away. Rollison rose to his feet and looked stupidly about him.

"I could manage a drink," he said; he was surprised at his thirst, at the weakness of his limbs. But he was getting better, for he heard Blanding distinctly when the man said: "Yes, of course," and saw him hurrying out of the bedroom. Others were bending over the huddled figure on the floor. "Of course," said Rollison, "Guy. He didn't expect it, he was too curious about the car. Sorry I had to destroy the evidence, Grice." he managed a smile. "I forgot he was so short, I meant to get his shoulder. What about—Race? You're looking after him?"

"I sent two men to watch him," said Grice. "Have you any definite news?"

"I think so. Who've you brought—oh, Lefroy. Good!" The berry-faced doctor was straightening up from Georgina, and he glanced sideways at Rollison, a humorous quirk at his lips. "I made a guess and said that Georgina took drugs," said Rollison. "Does she?"

"Is this Georgina?" asked Lefroy.

"Yes."

"She's quite prostrate," said Lefroy, "but as for an opinion—" he shrugged his shoulders and looked at her eyes, pulling the lids up.

"An opinion only," urged Rollison. "You won't have to take an oath on it."

"Then I don't think so," said Lefroy, "I've examined her pretty thoroughly, Grice." He was addressing the Superintendent and Rollison was reminding himself that many things had happened while he had been semi-conscious, and he had lost all count of time. "No, I don't think so," repeated Lefroy.

"Then you want Race," said Rollison, and grinned inanely. "Race for Race. But is it a charge? Falsely declaring that a patient is addicted to drugs? Georgina could swear a charge of defamation of character. Take a chance on it, will you?"

"We'll have him in for questioning," said Grice. He busied himself with one of the waiting men; the flashlights were going and they dazzled Rollison, for the room missed the sun and until then had been shadowy.

"Quite a party," said Rollison. "What about that drink, Grice?" He raised his voice, and Grice looked over his shoulder.

"Blanding—" he said, and paused.

Rollison said: "Yes. He went to get me a drink. How long has he been gone?" He stepped towards the door, adding sharply: "Too long. Oh, damn!" His knees began to bend and but for one of the policemen he would have fallen. As it was, he was led meekly to an easy chair and seated in it, after Grice had hurried out of the room in search of Blanding.

Near the chair, on a small table, was Georgina's handbag, lying open. Some visiting-cards were inside, but Rollison would not have touched them had not one been face downwards. On the reverse side were little drawings, of a top-hat, a monocle and a swagger cane.

Suddenly tense, he took it out; it was identical with the one which young Charmion had shown him.

Georgina had sent the card, had harrassed the younger Charmions in his name!

CHAPTER XX

THE EVASIVE DR. RACE

"Blanding?" asked Rollison. "Or no Blanding?"

"Ye-es," said Grice. "We've found him."

It was later that afternoon—so late that at Rollison's flat the curtains were drawn and the artificial light was dazzling enough to hurt his eyes; his head ached abominably, but he refused with petulant obstinacy to go to bed, so sat uncomfortably in an easy chair, with his left arm in a sling. He had been there for two hours, after being brought to the flat in a police car, and after Jolly and Fifi had received strict instructions as to what he should be allowed to do and not to do. Fifi appeared to have forgotten her own great trouble in Rollison's plight; to see him *hors de combat* seemed to horrify her, as if part of the world which she had thought secure had suddenly toppled about her.

Rollison gathered that Jolly would not be sorry when she had gone; even as he talked to Grice, who had just arrived, he could hear her scolding his man. He thought much more of Blanding, who had left the house instead of going to get Rollison's drink. He had, it proved, received a telephone message when he had reached the hall, and presumably had heard something which had made him hurry off.

"Where?" asked Rollison.

"He was picked up in Regent's Park," said Grice. "I put a call out for him, and his wife, as soon as I realized that he had gone."

"Prominent member of the Government found wandering in Regent's Park, was it?" asked Rollison, slowly. "Wandering is right?"

"Yes. He was quite distraught."

"Has he talked?"

"He's said very little, and he refused to answer questions."

"The man's a victim of this devilry, and he's badly hit. First his stepdaughter and then himself. What about Lady B.?"

"No trace," said Grice, briefly.

"The source of his trouble, I suppose? It sounds like a telephoned order to keep quiet or his wife will suffer, so he keeps quiet, but can't hide his distress. But there's something else. Why was Moor so anxious to kill Georgina—he did try, didn't he? What was that little pellet he popped into her mouth?"

"Enough morphine to kill half a dozen people."

"So her life was saved by my little finger," said Rollison, regarding the swollen member affectionately. "It was a bad jolt. I'd call Moor a decorative feature of the background and left it at that. Big mistake, and I realize it now—his story of the way he tried to get in touch with Georgina was pretty weak, and he was very persistent in his efforts to 'help'. Just too much the hopeless, helpless swain, if I'd cared to think about it that way. What does he say?"

Grice shook his head. "He won't say a word."

Although it was barely seven o'clock, Grice looked as if he needed a night's sound sleep. His eyes were glassy and he kept yawning, while he had not shaved that day, and now and again he rasped his stubble; dark stubble growing from his blemishless skin looked out of place—it was like looking at a woman who shaved but kept the fact a secret. He was ensconced in an arm-chair by Rollison's side, and at his side in turn there was a glass of grape-fruit cordial. By Rollison's side there was a silver tankard of ale, and he made a clumsy movement with his right hand to get at it.

"To their perdition!" he said, and drank. "Well, where are we? Not very far along?"

"I can't see much more than you know," said Grice.

"We haven't tied this side of the affair up with the Charmions, although I'm having them closely watched."

"Nicely said," admired Rollison. "Closely watched, when you might have been forgiven for hauling them in. All the haunts of vice are being equally well surveyed, I suppose? The Yard is the centre of an ever-widening circle, and dozens of lines lead from it to the satellites of Charmion."

Grice said, slowly:

"Still Charmion?"

"It has its roots in Charmion," said Rollison. "Whether he's still in it, we can't tell yet. Never was so much patience required by so many in whom a state of patience is a constant purgatory!"

"You sound almost good-humoured," said Grice, sourly.

The Toff grinned. "I wish I could return the compliment! On the whole, we can't grumble. They would have killed Georgina, because of what she knows, and she can surely know only what Hilda and Anderson discovered. So Georgina is very precious."

Grice said: "She was reluctant to talk to you, you say? Do you think it was because of the man Moor?"

"It could be," conceded Rollison, and hoped that the comment did not sound too glib. "How is she?"

"Lefroy doesn't think she'll be able to talk rationally for two or three days," said Grice, somberly. "They might be vital days. She has someone with her day and night, of course, and the moment she comes round we'll try to make her tell what she knows. Meanwhile, we're looking for Race and Lady Blanding. I agree with you that Blanding probably received a threatening telephone call. If we judge from what has happened before in this business, his wife is in danger and he will not make a statement because of it. The same method was applied to the Links."

"And almost certainly to Hilda Brent, who knew more than she told the Links, but dared not put it all into words." Said Rollison. "If Georgina can give us the key

170

when she comes round, Georgina herself could be in a healthier position." He knew that she could, the fact that she had acted in his name proved it; but Grice need know nothing of that yet. No one need know, not even Jolly, until he understood her motive.

Grice proved his weariness by snapping:

"Don't be a fool! She is watched night and day, with men outside her door and her window, and a nurse in the room. Nothing can happen to Georgina!"

"Touching faith," murmured Rollison. "However, the fact that it can doesn't mean that it will, and I'd rather rely on your men than anyone else, which no one would ever believe I would admit to a policeman! 'Two or three days'," he mused, "is a long time. It might even give them time to settle their affairs and disperse. We don't want them to disperse—"

"Confound it, who *are* they?" demanded Grice. "How many are there of them? What are they doing?"

Rollison said: "We've agreed that there's no murder without a motive; there's no crime without one, either. But the motive needn't be the usual one. I think—" he narrowed his eyes and went on in a gentle voice: "I may be wrong, Grice, but I think I see it now, from beginning to end. Operative word 'think', and I'll need to get the little cells working harder. So will you. After all," he went on, widening his eyes and lighting a cigarette with one hand, "you know as much about it as I do. I haven't kept back a single relative fact."

Grice said: "I suppose that means you don't propose to tell me what's in your mind?"

"Not yet," agreed the Toff, "because you're a policeman, and policemen have to bide by their most useful regulations, but regulations can sometimes be sidetracked with advantage. Which is my philosophy of criminal law!" He finished his beer and, with some difficulty, rose to his feet. "Hadn't you better get home and have a nap? You look worn out."

"I've got to go to the Yard and make my report," said Grice. He made no attempt to make Rollison change his mind, but there was a touch of bitterness in his voice as he went on: "Do you realize that this case has caused us more trouble than any single one for years? We're so busy these days that we've hardly time to do any one thing properly, and now—" He drew a deep breath. "The A.C. asked pointedly this afternoon whether it was my usual practice to send men running here and there at your behest"—Grice was so serious that he did not smile —"and I had the devil's own job to persuade him that whenever I've done so in the past it's been worth while."

"Ah!" said the Toff.

"And you say 'ah'!" complained Grice, bitterly.

"Well, yes," said the Toff. "I think you've put your finger on the spot."

Grice stared. "Just what do you mean?"

"No," said Rollison, stepping towards the kitchen, which was no longer filled with the argumentative voices of Jolly and Fifi, "the fruit isn't ripe enough for picking, yet; I may be quite wrong. Do you remember that I suggested we were riding for the biggest fall ever? Or words to that effect?"

"Yes," said Grice.

"Link that up with my more recent vapourings," said the Toff, "and see what happens."

Grice looked hard at him; although he did not press for more, he seemed less worried when he left the flat, promising to telephone should there be any development in the search for the elusive Dr. Race, and promising, also, to send word to Rollison of anything he was able to learn about the Blandings' doctor.

When he had gone, Rollison called for Jolly and received his man and Fifi together.

"Jolly, did you telephone to Hetfordshire?"

"Yes, sir. Lady Forrest has nothing else to tell us."

"Good! I couldn't believe that it would spread up there, but it's as well to know for certain. You've told Fifi the whole story?"

"But yes, m'sieu!" said Fifi, warmly, "I 'ave 'eard all of eet. I only wish that Shoe—" she paused, then shrugged

172

her shoulders and added quietly: "You will do all that ees possible, m'sieu, of that I am sure. There ees so much more of importance, also, an' you, your poor arm."

"My arm's all right," said the Toff hastily. "Fifi, you were fond of Hilda?"

"I was devoted to 'er."

"And there is Joe—" Rollison paused, seeming to weigh his words very carefully. Then abruptly: "Fifi, I don't think anyone else can help quite as well as you. It will be dangerous, but if you succeed"—he eyed her intently, seeing that blank expression in her brown eyes and wondering what was passing through her Gallic mind—"it will avenge Hilda, it will free Joe, and it will save Miss Scott and perhaps many others from serious harm."

"I am at your sairvice, m'sieu," said Fifi, with such unaffected dignity that Jolly glanced at her with approval. "Please, what ees eet that I do?"

"You go to see Charmion," said the Toff. "The Charmion you don't believe in, Fifi. You're wrong, and it is Charmion, and he is still clever, very clever. You understand that?"

"Yes, m'sieu."

"He will wonder whether you are telling him the truth, and you will have to convince him that you are," said Rollison. "If you fail—there will not be much chance, I think, for either you or Joe."

"Ees eet the truth I tell him, m'sieu?"

"No," said the Toff.

"Then I will convince 'eem," said Fifi.

"You'll leave here, soon, talking to yourself—in French will be best, but you can insert some English words. You will be very angry. All the way to his flat you will talk to yourself"—he spoke with simple directness which she could not fail to understand—"especially as you go up the stairs and wait for the door to open."

"That ees simple, m'sieu! Often, I talk to myself, when Shoe upsets me!"

173

"That's good," smiled the Toff. "Charmion will be there. You have to tell him that you and I have quarrelled—because I will not look for Joe. You are angry with me; you think that Charmion might, after all, know where Joe is. He will ask you what I am doing, of course, and you will tell him that I believe Joe is one of the rogues."

"M'sieu!" protested Fifi, "I—but no, I am sorry, thees ees what I tell Charmion!" For a moment her composure broke, but she regained it quickly.

"You will tell him that I believe Joe is working with the rogues," said Rollison, "and that I am very pleased with myself because I have killed a man named Guy and also arranged for the arrest of a man named Moor. You will remember the names?"

"Guy—Moor," repeated Fifi, parrot-like. "Yes, m'sieu."

"I am pleased with myself," repeated Rollison, "because I believe that it is all over bar shouting—try to remember the phrase, Fifi—'all over bar shouting'."

"All over bar shahting," said Fifi, and she might have been Joe Link talking. "Shoe, 'e often says that, m'sieu; eet will be easy to remember."

"Splendid!" said Rollison. "Now, Charmion will want to know what I am going to do. Tell him that I am going to see his wife and to find out whether she knows Sir Roland Blanding." He saw Jolly start, but kept his gaze on Fifi. "You have heard me discussing this with Jolly, of course. Say that I believe that Charmion's wife and Sir Roland Blanding knew each other, and that I can get at the final truth through them. Is that all clear, Fifi?"

"M'sieu, a moment!" exclaimed Fifi. She stared at him, her forehead wrinkled in concentration, her eyes intent. Then she drew a deep breath and began to speak. She repeated what the Toff had told her, almost word for word, repeating also the names of Guy, Moor, and Blanding. Only twice did the Toff need to prompt her, and when she had finished he nodded approvingly.

"I am pairfect, m'sieu? C'est bon! I weel make 'eem

174

believe it. But—" she frowned again, mercurial, emotional, tears now very close to her eyes. "Shoe, m'sieu—"

"If Charmion believes you, and if I am right in what I think, you will have Joe back," the Toff assured her, "but it will depend on how well you do it."

"I will do it pairfect, m'sieu! When do I begin?"

"You'd better have some supper," said the Toff, "and then get going."

"I do not need—" began Fifi.

"You might be a long time without a meal," said the Toff, "and so might I! Supper first, action afterwards. Will you get it, while I have a word with Jolly?"

She hurried off, making the floor shake beneath her weight, and, as if she realized that the Toff did not want her to hear what he said to Jolly, she closed the door firmly.

"So you think it is Charmion, sir?" Jolly said.

"I'm very nearly sure," admitted the Toff. "As for Blanding—" he shrugged his shoulders. "We'll see. We might call it the Great Illusion," he added softly. "If I'm right—"

"I have a feeling that you will be, sir," said Jolly.

"Yes. You're a help, you're always a help." Rollison smiled at him, and shifted his position, frowning down at his sling. "This arm isn't going to be."

"I suppose you're going to Mrs. Charmion's apartment?"

"Yes," said the Toff. "So, I think, will Charmion."

"Am I to come with you, sir?"

"I think you'd better follow me," said Rollison, slowly. "Bring a gun, we can never tell what might happen. I think Charmion will believe I'm too near, dangerously near, and that he'll try to finish it off there. It all depends," he added, quietly, "on Fifi." And then, in a sudden burst of exuberance, he began to hum the tune of *It All Depends On You*; he seemed very confident, yet beneath the confidence Jolly knew there was almost unbearable strain.

175

CHAPTER XXI

THE WIFE OF CHARMION

The Toff confounded his wounded arm.

It had been a nuisance while walking down the stairs of the Gresham Terrace flat and while finding a taxi, a greater one climbing into the cab, and still greater because he had not been able to sit back with any comfort. Wilberforce Mansions was a block of flats half-way up Putney Hill, to which he had been directed by a policeman whose large form had loomed up just after he had left the taxi. That was waiting nearby, its driver content with a pound note in his pocket and the promise of another if he waited.

Rollison entered the mansions, and found himself in a brightly illuminated foyer. A uniformed porter sat in a glass-encased office, and came out smartly as Rollison looked about him. The floors were carpeted, there was subdued wall-lighting in the passages, and the air of luxury which had puzzled him when he had first heard of it; somewhere he had failed to associate luxury flats with the picture of the dope-ridden wife of Charmion.

"Can I help you, sir?" asked the commissionaire.

"I want Flat 41," said Rollison. "What floor is it on?"

"The second, sir. Shall I take you up?" The man looked at the sling, and, without waiting for an answer, walked towards the lift, which was standing open. "Better to-night than last night, sir, isn't it?"

"Yes," said Rollison, and as the iron gates clanged to, asked: "Do you know the flats well?"

"Yessir—like me own 'and," declared the other, an oldish, well-preserved man with a nut-cracker face. "Been 'ere ever since they was put up, sir. I know every tenant, noo an' old, sir."

"Is a Sir Roland Blanding one of them?" asked Rollison.

"No, sir, no one o' that name at all lives 'ere."

"I must have made a mistake," said Rollison, and when the man looked alarmed he added hastily: "Oh, I still want Flat 41, but someone told me that the Blandings live here. You're sure? A tall, good-looking, rather florid-faced man—red-faced and weather-beaten, that is. A complexion rather like your own," he added, as the lift came to a standstill.

"Several people *might* be described like that, sir," said the commissionaire, discreetly.

"His wife," said Rollison, "is a tall, remarkably beautiful woman—" He described Lady Blanding well enough for anyone who knew her well to recognize her at once. The man shot him a quick, suspicious glance and said, blank-faced:

"I don't reckernize the lady, sir."

"Are you sure?" asked Rollison. He had put some one pound notes in his right side pocket, so that he could get at them easily; he took one out. The commissionaire glanced at it, and then at Rollison's face.

"*Quite* sure, sir," he said, expressionlessly.

"Then I must be wrong, mustn't I?" asked Rollison, amiably. "But take this, for being discreet." He put the pound note into the man's hand and turned quickly away from the lift, following an arrow indicating 'Flats 35-58'. The commissionaire stood staring after him and the Toff whistled gently, believing that the other had recognized the description of one or the other of the Blandings, but that he was a loyal servant to the tenants of the block.

A clock in one of the flats chimed ten.

He had taken nearly three-quarters of an hour to get to Putney, and Fifi, by the time he had left Gresham Terrace, must have been at Charmion's flat for nearly three-quarters of an hour. If he were right, Charmion would not lose a lot of time coming here. He reached Number 41, paused, and then rang the bell. There was

177

no immediate response, but after a second ring the door opened.

"Who's that?" The voice rose upwards, like a being in torment; a narrow face beneath an untidy mop of hair showed by the door, which was opened only a few inches. "Who's that?"

"I want to see Mrs. Charmion," said the Toff, inserting his foot in the door.

"She ain't—" began the woman with the mop of hair, only to step back as the Toff went forward. She glared at him, her little, cunning eyes wide open. The Toff closed the door and looked at her, without speaking. Her hands fluttered and her pinched features went pale. Rollison judged from her swollen eyes and the pallor about her lips that she was no stranger to drugs; she had the white, pinched look at the nostrils which betrayed the habitual sniffer of cocaine. He judged her to be in the early fifties, although she looked older. She was dressed in an ill-fitting tweed suit, with patched carpet slippers on her feet; her hands were thin, a network of ugly veins.

"What do you mean by forcing your way in?" Her quavering voice was complaining, but she did it automatically; she was surprised at nothing, probably she had expected him.

The Toff said: "Where's Mrs. Charmion?"

"She's asleep," the woman said, "fast asleep; it would be cruel to wake her up, that it would."

"Yes," said the Toff. "Life can be cruel. It doesn't seem to have treated you too well. How long have you served Mrs. Charmion?"

"More'n seven years," she whined, "more'n seven years, I been a faithful servant, I have. More'n seven long years!" She glanced towards a closed door on the right of the small entrance hall; the Toff understood why she had not made more voluble protests—she had received instructions to let him in and to talk like this. He put his right hand to his pocket, where he carried his automatic as well as the pound notes, and said:

"I want to ask you one or two questions."

178

The woman sent another scared look towards the door, licking her colourless lips but saying nothing. Rollison wondered whether, even now, he had made a mistake. He did not question his assumptions, but thought that Charmion might decide to kill him there and then and take what consequences there might be.

Then the door opened.

He pretended to be surprised, but although his heart beat fast it was mostly with satisfaction; for it was Charmion, and obviously the man intended to talk.

It was the Charmion who had been at Gresham Terrace and talked so plausibly, but he had all the confidence which he had shown when talking to his brother and sister-in-law. His face looked less drawn, perhaps because of the twisted smile at his lips. His eyes were no longer lack-lustre; it was much easier for the Toff to recognize the man as he used to be.

"So you've got here, Rollison?"

"Why, hallo," said the Toff. "I didn't think I'd find you here. I thought your wife wasn't on your visiting list."

"You aren't always right," said Charmion. "What do you want here?"

Rollison put his head on one side, took off his hat and threw it on a small table, and then stepped towards Charmion, with his right hand in his pocket. Charmion moved back into the other room. It was a lounge, well furnished in modern fashion by someone who had good taste and ample means; there was an atmosphere of snug luxury.

No one else was in there.

"Well, your real wife looked after herself even if she forgot you!" said Rollison, heartily. "Or—" he sat on the arm of an easy chair and smiled into the man's eyes— "didn't she? Your story was very plausible, but have you heard the old story of the leopard and its spots?" He leaned forward and took a cigarette from a box on a small occasional table, and struck a match. Charmion stared, his body tense. "You know," said Rollison, easily, "you've prepared some unpleasant surprises for me, of

179

course, but I've one or two up my sleeve for you. Fifi convinced you, didn't she? She didn't need a lot of coaching, either."

Charmion seemed to shrink within himself; his eyes were angry and his lips curled; an oath hovered on them, but faded into the corners of the room as Rollison said:

"The first trick, I think. Fifi simply worked to get you here, and it was very nicely done."

Charmion said, softly:

"You may think that you are clever, Rollison, but—"

"*I'm* not clever!" disclaimed the Toff, hastily. "I've been nearer to being a fool than ever in my life, but you made your own mistakes, too. You carried the hoaxing just too far, laying on the suspense too thick. You shouldn't have instructed your brother to leer at me as he left your flat; I was quite sure, when I thought over that, that you'd arranged the quarrel for my benefit, that it had all been planned beforehand, in the hope of keeping me guessing." He shook his head, sadly. "And you shouldn't have put flavouring in that whisky at the Parrot Club. You thought they were the artistic touches, but actually they were the flaws."

"You are talking a lot of drivel!" snapped Charmion.

"Oh, no," said the Toff. "Hard facts. It's a pity you didn't spend your undoubted ingenuity on something more worthwhile. As it is—" he shrugged—"I told Fifi enough to make you think that I was dangerously close to the truth. How's this for mind-reading: 'He's too near for comfort; I'll see him at Putney and try to convince him that he's wrong about Blanding, but if he doesn't seem convinced I'll kill him on his way home'? Not far out?" asked the Toff, and drew his hand, quite casually, from his pocket; the wall-lighting shone on the grey steel of his automatic, and Charmion glanced once towards it. "Not bad?" repeated the Toff, laconically. "I thought you'd agree. This is the final act, Charmion."

"You are quite mad!" snapped Charmion.

"It's too late to try to convince me of any different setup," said the Toff, gently. "You see, it's all fitted in very well. This woman here, this raddled harridan—*your* wife? Would you marry a woman twenty years your senior when you could have married any one of the hundred most beautiful women in England? The first major flaw, you see—this woman you said was your wife was nothing of the kind. You selected someone to act the part, someone whose mind was blurred with drugs and who was not likely to betray you. You might even have married her bigamously before you left for Dartmoor, but that's neither here nor there. All the same—you *were* married, Charmion. I've checked up all the necessary details. You married a charming and beautiful woman, a widow—*named Scott*. Didn't you, Charmion?"

He had never held serious doubts, from the moment 'Lady Blanding' had left the Portman Place house in the taxi and Guy had been so anxious to make sure that she got away, although he had checked nothing. The blazing hatred in Charmion's eyes gave him all the confirmation he could desire. There was no 'Lady Blanding'; she was Charmion's real wife.

Charmion did not move.

Perhaps it was the gun in Rollison's hand which kept him rigid, his eyes burning with the hatred which had been conceived, seven years before, in the dock at the Old Bailey. He still retained the trick of immobility which made it seem that he was about to spring, that he would do great harm when he did so.

Rollison said:

"Your wife 'married' Blanding. Some people take bigamy as it comes, it's treated too leniently in many courts. Anyone completely amoral—anyone who could marry you, that is, knowing what you were—would think little of it. You were in Dartmoor, your wife was footloose, Blanding fell in love with her—and he was a wealthy man. I haven't the slightest doubt that you were party to it, either before or after the event. I've no doubt that she's wrung a fortune out of Blanding."

When Charmion said nothing, Rollison went on:

181

"Georgina discovered it, of course. It was more than she could believe; she just could not credit that her mother was capable of such a thing, and yet she was afraid. So she wanted the truth to come out, although she would not take any active part in helping it—except to warn me. Georgina deserved a better mother, Charmion."

Still Charmion did not move.

The revelation of Rollison's theory must have made him seethe; his immobility made Rollison feel sure that someone else was in the flat. There was danger in the very air; Charmion would try to make sure that he carried this story only to the grave. The tension mounted, making it difficult for him to concentrate on Charmion's face, but he contrived to, and went on, in a gentle, mocking voice:

"Your wife really made me understand, when she invited me to go to see Georgina. You see, I had told the manager of the Parrot Club that it would all be over in forty-eight hours. He told 'Lady Blanding', of course, since she was on the committee, and then it reached you. You had to find out whether I had talked for the sake of it or whether I was near the truth, and you thought the best way to find out was to persuade me to see Georgina. Guy was in the wardrobe to listen to the questions I asked, to put an end to Georgina and I if the need arose. I stung him when I talked of Race. There was a big mistake on Dr. Race's part, too. He was with you in the plot, and was too prompt in telling Blanding that Georgina took drugs, for when I saw her again this afternoon I realized that I had been wrong; she didn't take drugs, she was suffering from great emotional strain. I'd suggested drugs to Blanding, and Race decided that it would be simplest if he said 'yes'. A really grave mistake, wasn't it?"

When Rollison stopped, there was no sound in the room, but the tension was not caused only by his words; some hidden presence, the suspicion that unseen eyes were watching him, the imminence of an attempt to kill him, all played a part. But he continued to eye Charmion, and went on, softly, because he wanted to hear any movement that might be made in the next room.

"Hilda Brent learned something of it—I suspect that she knew this woman supposed to be your wife, and learned through her. Anderson—I was very slow when I heard what Anderson said to you: he'd just seen your supposed wife, and when he told you that you allowed him in. He'd learned that she wasn't your wife, probably he had also learned who the lucky woman was"—he could not keep the sneer out of his voice—"and as he'd seen her, he could only have learned it from these flats. 'Lady Blanding' also has a flat here, Charmion, hasn't she?"

Charmion drew in a short, hissing breath.

"The commissionaire here is very loyal, but just an ordinary man. With what he didn't say and what Anderson did, the story builds up! As for Dr. Race—I haven't seen the elusive doctor, but doubtless he knew that Lady Blanding had no right to her name or position, hence his introduction to the magic circle. How am I doing?" Rollison asked.

Charmion broke his long silence with a soft:

"You were worth fighting, Rollison."

"Generous of you," murmured the Toff. "So were you. So Race did know about her bigamy. Perhaps her carelessness encouraged him to muscle in?"

"It—did," said Charmion.

"That's fine!" said Rollison. He thought he saw the handle of the door turn, and calculated the chances of firing as it opened and at the same time preventing Charmion from moving. "What of Moor? You see, I don't know everything."

"Moor was a junior member of my League," said Charmion, "and he remained faithful."

"A grievous thing, when man has faith in base ideals," said Rollison, ironically. "And, of course, you made him dance attendance on Georgina, because you were afraid of what she had learned. He was to find out what she

183

knew and what she proposed to do. Of course! That was one of the reasons why she could not tell me openly. And she was followed when she came to see me at the Kettledrum; the card with your magic name was thrust into her coat so that she knew the risk she took if she betrayed her mother. What a choice for a girl! But she tried, Charmion, although she would speak no word against your woman. And—" he paused, again thinking that the handle turned, but the door remained closed. "Blanding is an innocent victim, of course. I'm sorry for him. That was what he was told over the telephone, why he will not speak—he cannot believe it of her, of course; he is sick to his soul."

Charmion said: "You will be more sick."

"I don't think so," said Rollison, but he saw in the words a threat of coming action; his nerves were stretched taut as he looked deliberately towards the door.

It opened, without warning.

Charmion's real wife stood there, even then with an obscure smile on her lovely face. She wore tweeds, had not a hair out of place; obviously she had just made up. Although looking at Rollison, she spoke to Charmion. In her hand, pointing at Rollison, was an automatic.

"So he's won, Gilbert?"

"No," said Charmion, "he won't live to tell the story."

Rollison said, mendaciously: "It's told; all Grice wants are the details, and he isn't far away."

"You won't live to tell the story," said Charmion, "even if we have to die with you."

CHAPTER XXII

THE GREAT ILLUSION

"Histrionics apart," said Rollison, with forced lightness, "it's an *impasse*."

"I shall kill you," said Charmion, dispassionately. "Dr. Race is in the room behind you, Rollison. He has had a flat here for a long time, although not under his own name. He and my wife"—he looked at the woman, and Rollison could well believe that he loved her; it was a strange thought, warping his whole idea of Charmion, whom he had imagined would live and die for himself alone—"used it when it was convenient."

Rollison mused: "The commissionaire thought there was more in it than that, of course. A useful man."

"Don't waste my time talking of fools!"

"Not a fool," said the Toff, gently, "an ordinary man and an honest and loyal one—your faith in the common man is sadly wanting, Charmion. You've taken too many people for fools because of your previous experience. With your gilded tongue and your wonderful looks you fooled them—but a man and woman who are fooled are not necessarily fools, there's a difference you might see one day." He talked swiftly, backing slowly towards a corner of the room, to make sure that he could not be taken by surprise. "And now—for the Great Illusion!"

"If you think you are gaining time for yourself, forget it," said Charmion. "I shall be warned when the police arrive outside—*if* they come. I know that there are two watching the front door now, but they don't matter—when the end comes it will come quickly." He spoke without a trace of emotion, but the expression in his eyes carried Rollison back again seven long years to the courtroom at the Old Bailey—all this, including the Great Illusion, had started then.

"I'll take my chance," said the Toff. "You've probably heard it rumoured that I like to hear myself talk. The Great Illusion," he added, gently. "You had these clubs, innocent clubs behind good cover—your brother and his wife ran them, and *your* wife helped. Race supplied the drugs, but always in small quantities. The only real addict in this case is the woman you claimed as your wife. You had your troupe of performing parrots"—he sneered the words—"and your waiters. You had the whole thing set, it was another League of Physical Beauty—physical degradation would suit it better!—in embryo. You allowed a few poor girls to be caught by the police, you let one of the little men sell one the stuff and be identified, you drew police attention to the Parrot Club, knowing that they could not get past it, because there *was* nothing. Only one of the ten little men was named Guy, only one of the waiters followed me. There were too many for a correct identification, you played safely behind that. You built a great conception of a powerful drug-trafficking organization, you—"

"You've said enough," interpolated Charmion.

"Let him go on," said the woman, smiling as if she were in a different world, yet holding her gun steady and with the drop on Rollison. "Let us see how much he does know."

Rollison said, sardonically:

"You're quite an artist. But is there much more? You set the stage but made it impossible for the police to trace anything farther than the club. There was no great vice in the members, only enough to keep the police on a stretch and to make them search for the real organization, the real power behind the precious scheme—*which did not really exist.*"

The woman said: "You see, Gilbert? He knows."

"I know," said Rollison, close to the corner now and wary, although he did not think that they would make a mistake; he saw no chance of escaping, and was surprised

186

that it affected him so little. "You had to kill Hilda Brent because of what she knew about your supposed wife, and you attempted to frame me. You drew attention to yourself, only to divert it. The really Machiavellian mind! You thought that you had me on the run, confused and apprehensive—and you weren't far wrong! You added every little touch you could to make confusion worse confounded. You watched as the police went here and there, using more and more men, straining their resources to the limit.

"You watched while I tested each detail and tried to see the truth, but you thought your illusion was perfect. You had the police looking for a dope-ring that didn't exist. You had me searching for the same organization, which was quite brilliant. You told Anderson fanciful stories, making him think the organization existed. You wanted revenge on me, on Hilda Brent, on the law that had cost you seven years of your life. You planned and plotted it in jail, your brother and the women put it into operation while you were inside, because you thought it could never then be traced to *you*. But for the other affair, with Blanding, you might have succeeded, but you had to mix cold-blooded crime with the grandiose hoax bred out of the noxious bitterness in your mind." He paused, knowing that he still lacked the final truth, the Blanding side to Charmion's plot. "You were influenced by the fact that you thought I knew of the Blanding gambit. I didn't, you know. I didn't work on your brother, either."

"No," said Charmion, "I only realized that to-day."

"Georgina—" began Rollison.

Charmion said, softly: "Georgina thought that her mother was being blackmailed by my brother. She knew of you because you had helped the man Marchant. She had cards like yours printed, she sent telegrams, she telephoned, all in your name. And she completely deceived me, Rollison, I thought it was you, and I had to try to get you off the scent, I wanted to protect—my wife." He glanced at the woman, then looked back at Rollison.

187

"What you didn't know was that my fortune *was* lost, soon after I went to prison—it was no one's fault, just bad investments."

Rollison stared, with a sudden flash of understanding.

"You see?" murmured Charmion. "My wife"—again he looked at her—"was importuned by Blanding, who lost his head over her. But he is an upright man"—Charmion sneered—"and nothing short of marriage would suit him. So she married him and fleeced him, and built up my fortune again. Her daughter knew what she was doing but put it down to blackmail. I had to divert your attention. I began months ago, when first I thought you were getting curious, after getting reports at Dartmoor. And—it wasn't you, it was Georgina!"

Rollison said: "Nice work, Georgina!"

She had grown desperate, of course, suspecting the real truth at last, had known she must find a way of introducing him to the affair, had chosen the telephone call and the mystifying story; but afterwards the situation had got too much for her, for Charmion had learned that she was approaching the Toff and had started to work on her.

Nothing was left unexplained.

Charmion said, slowly:

"I should have waited for a dark night and shot you, Rollison, as I'd once planned to do. But I knew your methods, I was afraid of what information you might leave behind, I thought you suspected the truth. The other was more fitting, too. I wanted you accused of Hilda Brent's murder, to hear the sordid details brought out in court. I planned that you should have too much on your mind to worry about the Blandings and Georgina."

"You were thorough," Rollison admitted, "revenge on Hilda and on me, and your fortune rebuilt. A man and a girl suffering the torment of the damned meant nothing to you, but the framing failed, you had to improvise and began to lose your grip."

"The police should never have let you go!" rasped Charmion. "Nor would they have done had I been able to get at that taxi-driver and stop his mouth! But *I* haven't lost, Rollison. You're going to die in any case."

"The flat will be quite a shambles, won't it?" asked the Toff.

He heard a shout from the next room, and at first thought that Jolly had arrived. But it was the woman with the mop of grey hair, who shouted again. Someone swore at her, a woman whose voice was thick and hoarse. The door opened and the speaker appeared; her face was raddled, there were dark bags beneath her eyes, which glittered with an unholy light.

Rollison believed that she had always thought herself to be Charmion's wife; but now she had overheard the truth.

She screamed: "Charmion! Look what you've done to me, look what you've done!" She raised her scraggy hands, then uttered on a lower note: "I *hate* you, Charmion, you and this—this Jezebel!"

She turned and flung herself at the other woman, and so complete was the surprise that the automatic was sent to the floor. The beautiful face of the younger woman was suddenly scarred by weals, oozing blood, scratched deep into her cheeks. And as they fought, Charmion swung towards the Toff, who reached him and struck him with his sound hand, still holding his gun. He turned as the other door opened and Dr. Race appeared—to stop short when he saw the gun in Rollison's hand.

"Stop the women!" ordered Rollison.

Race moved to obey, dazedly—and while he was trying, while the drug-ridden dupe of Charmion was taking the revenge which put so perfect a finishing touch to the fantastic case, while the woman with the mop of hair began to moan and cry in the doorway, there was a hammering on the passage door and Jolly's voice was raised.

Rollison, more biddable now that it was all over, although somewhat restive because he was in bed, looked at Grice on the following morning. The Superintendent

189

had just read back to him a statement which he had dictated after the shambles at the Putney flat.

Fast upon Jolly's arrival the police had come; by then the woman who had known a living death yet come to life again in so great a fury, had lost consciousness. It was known that she had believed herself the wife of Charmion and had heard the truth when the Toff had spoken. Of the beauty who was known as Lady Blanding there had been only a shivering, bleeding wreck, who had broken down completely. She had been arrested with Charmion.

Charmion's brother and his wife had also been arrested; they had been caught on their way to a house at Barking, where Fifi's Joe had been found, uninjured—used, like Fifi, to add more realism to the Great Illusion. There had been a tearful reunion between him and Fifi.

"And that's all?" said Grice, slowly.

The Toff raised his eyebrows.

"Aren't you ever satisfied? If you want more—" he shrugged—"but perhaps I did forget one or two details. For instance, why I told Charmion that I thought Blanding was in it, not his 'wife'; I wanted him to think, right to the end, that I had been hoodwinked and that I believed in his reformation. Had I mentioned the woman he would have seen through it—he missed very little." Rollison took a cigarette from a bedside table, then asked: "What did Race have to say?"

"He was in it for what he could get—he started by blackmailing Lady Blanding." Grice smiled, crookedly. "I still find myself thinking of her as that."

"Don't we all?" asked Rollison, and added slowly: "She angled for me to go to see Georgina, of course, to find out just what I had learned." He paused. "I missed some fairly obvious things, you know. The association between the younger Charmion and Blanding's own daughter—the younger Charmion traded on what he knew about the stepmother to wrong the daughter. I should have seen that as evidence that the Blandings and Charmion were connected. Georgina, of course, was at

190

school at the time of the trial and the genuine marriage. Then she began to understand." He drew on his cigarette. "Well, we shouldn't grumble now. Fifi's happy—by the way, she's taking Hilda's children, and—"

Grice smiled: "You're seeing that they won't be in need!"

Rollison shrugged and asked: "How is Georgina?"

"Better than she was," said Grice.

"I wish there could be something more cheerful for her to come back to," said Rollison. "At least, Blanding will do all he can to help her. I like that man. The only thing I'd like to know," added the Toff, "is whether Georgina *did* hear that conversation at the Savoy, and decide that it would be the best way of attracting me, or whether she thought of it before?"

"You won't worry her with that, surely?" asked Grice.

"No," said Rollison, "but all the same I'd like to know. Teddy Marchant is supposed to have insisted that she should tell me, but she might have taken his name in vain. It's ten thousand pities about Teddy. I think Blanding was right in one respect, Georgina was fond of him."

"It seems so," said Grice, who left soon afterwards.

Later in the day, Jolly tapped softly on the door; Rollison was awake, and reading from Browning, a sedative of which he could never have enough. Diana, who had been telephoned and told what had happened, had given him the copy he was reading.

There was an air of suppressed excitement about Jolly.

"Are you—" he began.

"I am," said the Toff.

"Oh, fine!" cried another voice, and a man came storming in, a fair-haired, rugged, anxious-faced man whose uniform was singed and whose right hand was heavily bandaged. "Rolly," he said urgently, "I've been trying to see Georgina—you know, Georgina Scott—but they won't let me in. Someone mentioned your name—what's the matter with her?" He was on tenterhooks as he stared down at Rollison, his good hand raised.

Rollison drew a deep, wondering breath.

191

"Teddy, you oaf! I thought you—"

"I had a spot of luck," said Teddy Marchant, off-handedly. "But never mind that, what about Georgina?"

"She'll be all right, now," said Rollison, happily. "But you've a job on your hands, Teddy. D'you feel like tackling it?"

"For Georgina, I'd—" began Teddy, and then broke off, a little abashed. "Well, you know what I mean."

"I do," admitted the Toff. "Teddy, sit down, and I'll tell you a story—but before I start, tell me this: were you with Georgina in the Savoy a few days ago, when a man mentioned my name?"

"Was I?" Teddy stared, blankly. "No."

Rollison chuckled.

"You've certainly got a job on your hands; Georgina has a mind and uses it!" He grew more sober. "Make some tea, Jolly, will you?" he asked, and then settled down to tell Marchant all that was necessary, feeling much happier for Georgina.

Weeks later, he learned that even Blanding had not known how his 'wife' was cheating him, that a fortune in money and jewels and stocks and shares had been surreptitiously stolen or transferred to her, to replace what Charmion had lost.

"Had Georgina told me," Rollison said to Jolly, "we would have approached it from a different angle. Instead, she hoped my name alone would be enough to frighten them."

"And wasn't it, sir?" asked Jolly.